Desires and Deceptions

Catherine Burr

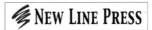 NEW LINE PRESS

DESIRES AND DECEPTIONS
Copyright © 2006 by Catherine Burr

ISBN trade paperback: 1-892851-02-4

Library of Congress Card Number: 2005936042

This book was printed in the USA

Cover artwork design by Larry Wall & Kathleen Russell

For inquires or to order additional copies of this book, contact:
New Line Press.
www. newlinepress.com

10 9 8 7 6 5 4 3 2 1

Dedicated to the memory of
my brother, Raymond.

Acknowledgements

This book came to fruition by the dedication of two people, Kathleen Russell and Larry Wall. Their enthusiastic support brought this project from a desire to a realized goal.

My gratitude goes out to my critique partner who listened patiently as I read page after page, and who kept the coffee pot on.

I thank my parents, Dorothy and Cliff Wall, who were always willing to read yet another chapter, and who taught me to believe in myself and go for my dreams.

Thank you to my sister, Beverly Rose Hopper, for lending a listening ear. To Martin, Neil, and Emily - you enrich my life.

To my sons, Tim and Daniel - love you guys.

To Timothy, thank you with love.

Always,
Catherine

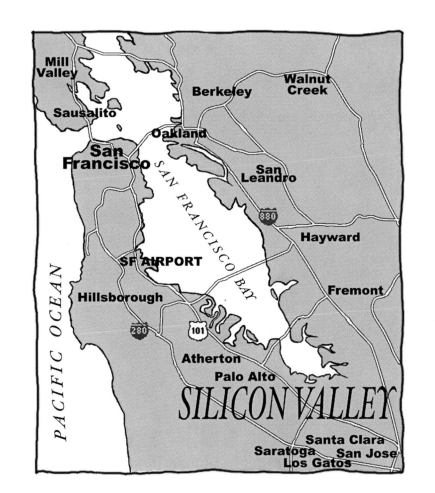

Chapter One

Marisa pulled her Louis Vuitton suitcase out from the top shelf of her walk in closet knowing that she should have packed the night before. Procrastination had always been her weakness, but this time she had a valid excuse – the murder. A reason that burned so deep into her soul that she would abandon her exquisite home in beautiful Saratoga, California, an affluent Silicon Valley suburb nestled against the Santa Cruz mountains, where the average price of a home was out of reach for anyone but the wealthy.

It was before seven in the morning. Not Marisa McKenzie's best time of day, and now as she took a moment to savor her strong black coffee, she wondered what in the hell she was doing. If only there was a pause button that she could press, so the events of the past twenty-four hours would stop replaying over and over in her mind.

Reaching into the pocket of her denim cut-offs, ones that hugged her well-toned hips as if they'd been custom fit, she pulled out an elasticized scrunchy. She gathered her long dark hair, the color of a moonless night, into a ponytail. If only she'd been able to look into a crystal ball. She would've seen that their time together didn't mean forever. She wondered how long the secret would remain just that. How long until her family, the Valley -- the world, learned the truth?

She walked over to the wall and turned on the intercom.

"Girls, are you getting ready? We don't have much time."

Down the hall, the grandfather clock struck seven, the chimes echoed throughout their picturesque home.

"Girls! You hear me?"

"We know mother." Their youthful voices were harmonic, as if singing in the choir for the private school they attended – rather, used to attend.

"When we get there, can we go to Rodeo Drive?" Sarah the shopper yelled out, as she sat cross-legged on the floor of the media room, the remote control glued to her fingers as she switched between MTV and the Cartoon Network.

"Is Daddy coming with us?" Elizabeth asked in between bites of Cheerios.

Marisa chose to ignore the inquiries. Too many questions. Too few answers. "Just get ready girls. Please." Her voice cracked as if she were a teenage boy going through puberty. "And get the cat's stuff ready too," she added. God forbid if that shedding ball of fur would be left behind. Poor thing would never be fed again.

The radio was tuned to a San Francisco based AM news talk station. Normally she enjoyed listening to the wisecracking duo who delivered the daily morning news with an air of light-heartedness, but this morning, for the moment, it was mere background noise.

The image of the gold ring in the jeweler's box sitting on her kitchen table was foremost in her mind. The small velvet container held the ring captive inside.

Reaching for her mug, she sipped her coffee and closed her eyes hoping the image of the tainted ring would go away. Would the Guatemalan blend clear her brain fog? Taking a sip, she forced herself to focus on what to pack, as time was of the essence.

In the past she was discriminating in her selection of clothing but this time was different. This time she would not spend time laying out coordinating outfits. This time she would only pack comfort clothes. She would no longer fret over what to pack, ever again. She was only taking what she needed and would fit into one suitcase. The rest of her things could be sent for later … or maybe not.

Marisa shook her head clear of the mindless fashion clutter and packed a couple of sweaters, one black strapless dress, three casual dresses, and a couple of sweatshirts and two pairs of jeans.

Next, she started clearing off the top of her dresser where she kept her favorite mementos. She could not leave without these, and she would never trust a mover with them. They weren't just souvenirs, they represented her life.

Sure, she felt guilty about taking the coral from the reef off Maui, but she was so excited, and in love on that trip, that she wanted a solid remembrance. The purple glass vase she had watched being hand blown in a little village in Italy; a Japanese doll she had bought in Tokyo; a dried jasmine flower that had long since lost its scent; and of course, the two clay hand-prints that her girls each made in kindergarten, both of them were considered by her to be priceless pieces of art.

Marisa wrapped each of these treasures in tissue and packed them in between her clothes until there was only one memento left. A white porcelain figurine about eight inches tall of a woman holding two infants in her arms and it was her favorite. She picked up the statuette, turned it upside down, and removed the note from a hole in the bottom. She carefully unfolded the note and read it for what seemed like the thousandth time. It had once offered her so much comfort, but now as she read it, she realized it was meaningless.

"Darling, I am so sorry about the baby. Always remember that I love you. Please know that we are a perfect family, just the way we are. Love, J."

Marisa's eyes started to tear but she quickly wiped the salty moisture away. She didn't have time for a trip down memory lane now. The longer she lingered, the more she realized she had to hurry, she had to get out of the house, out of town. Fast.

In the beginning, she and Joshua wanted the same things, but it was the road getting there that Marisa was not prepared for. She did not know in the beginning that the land of opportunity, the land of gold, the town of Silicon, could so easily turn to rust.

Needing a mental distraction, Marisa turned up the volume of the radio. A news bulletin came on about a Silicon Valley figure having been found dead. She missed the name of who it was, but would have been both shocked and relieved if she had.

She turned the radio off and crawled under the covers of her bed. Clutching the figurine to her breast, she let her mind drift back, back to the beginning ...

Chapter Two

Years Earlier

"Mom! Mom. You're not going to believe what happened at school today." Marisa shouted with happiness as she burst through the kitchen door of her parent's small tract house.

Her mother could see it in Marisa's joyful green eyes that something very special had happened. "Sit down and tell me about it," she said, placing a plate of freshly baked oatmeal cookies on the table.

"What is it, dear?" She asked, pouring Marisa a glass of milk.

Marisa bit into a cookie and with crumbs falling down her chin started to tell her mother the good news, "Ethan is having a party!"

"Oh really?"

"Yeah. He invited me and everything, by the way mom, what is a bar mitzvah?"

"Well, a bar mitzvah is--"

"You can tell me later, mom. Right now, I want to talk about my dress. All the girls are buying new ones. I want one, too. Please."

"I don't know about buying one but I could sew you a beautiful dress."

"Oh. No Mom. Please. Can't we buy a new dress? Just this once?"

Marisa's mother shook her head. "I don't know. We're on a budget … But I'll tell you what," she said, while taking a bite of her own cookie, "I'll talk to your father about it when he gets home." She always ate when she was nervous, and now, the thought of her daughter venturing out into the world of parties and anything reeking of socio-economic class distinction made her very hungry.

"Let me know as soon as dad gets home."

Her mother smiled, "I will. In the meantime, go do your homework like a good girl."

Chapter Three

The Santa Clara Valley that Marisa's father, Charlie Taft, had come to know and love was now changing before his eyes. Orchards were being torn down to make way for indoor shopping malls and the new, sprawling computer companies. Noticeably, the groundwork was being laid for a division between the haves and the have-nots of Santa Clara Valley.

The valley that Charlie Taft knew was fading and reinventing itself, as *Silicon Valley*. Charlie was not ready for this change. He missed the valley's orchards that provided fruit to eat and a lush green beauty to admire. The local canneries were in danger of being closed. With them closed, the sweet scent of tomatoes wafting in the air was being replaced with a thick blanket of brown smog. The smog would make him sneeze, and it was a rare day in the valley to see Mount Hamilton, a wondrous view he admired. For Charlie, all the new really meant less, and he didn't want any part of it.

Charlie had a difficult time providing for his family which consisted of his wife Cassie, his son Johnny, now a Marine and away at the war in Viet Nam, and his darling, Marisa, the baby of the family.

In spite of their financial difficulties, Charlie and Cassie spent their married days happily living on love and an incarnate carnal desire for each other. They only aspired to make enough money -- to get by.

Although he knew a true peace and oneness in his being, he held a deep concern about his precious Marisa. He knew in his heart that he had made a mistake by bringing her that day – the day he took her to work on the … estate. He remembered one day in particular, the day when Marisa's life seemed to take on a new purpose and new meaning. It was the day he invited her to go along with him and she came back home with newfound wants and newfound desires.

Marisa saw things that day, things that had been non-existent to her before then. She saw things that day that she could only begin to dream of. Starting with the houses, houses like she had never seen before. Marisa squinted the sun out of her eyes as she strained to read the brass plaques hung on ivy covered, stonewalls.

She was astonished and stunned by the fact that her father had never once told her of this grandiose world, this ebullient display that she was witnessing now, first hand. She felt betrayed. Like he had deliberately kept this splendor hidden from her, like some secret. The only world she had known up to then, was her little world and her suburban neighborhood.

As they drove through the quiet streets of Atherton, Marisa simply marveled, everything was bigger and more marvelous than anything she had ever seen before; even the trees, they seemed to have more leaves and seemed greener.

They soon arrived at the mansion whose grounds he was working that day. He stopped the truck just outside the iron gates. Charlie stuck his tan muscular arm out the window and pressed the intercom button and the massive black wrought iron gates swung open.

To Marisa, the house looked more like a museum. Marisa jumped out of the truck and ran up to a window with a burgundy canopy. She wasn't quite tall enough to see in and had to jump up and down to get a glimpse inside. For a moment, she forgot who she was, for a moment she forgot that she was just a little girl with nothing, and time stood still. She blocked out the roaring sound of the leaf blower her dad was using across the driveway, and saw a life she wanted.

Charlie looked up from his leaf blower and yelled out to her, "What are you doing Mari? Get away from those windows, you don't need anything in there."

On the trip home that evening, Marisa was quiet. After being shown what life could offer, Marisa sat in their rusty, dirt-covered, noisy old pickup truck and meditated on her day. In her mind, they were leaving a world of splendor for the ugliness and common of her everyday life.

Marisa had a dazed look on her face and did not say a word almost the entire drive back home. And then, almost home, she proclaimed, "Daddy, I want to live like that one day."

Charlie couldn't answer as he knew then it had been a lapse in judgment by bringing her with him. He had just wanted to spend some time with her, and now he was sorry, so very sorry.

"I want inside of that world. More than anything."

"No, you don't Marisa. Just take my word on this. Money does not your heart make."

Chapter Four

Marisa spent the next few weeks determined to change her life. She knew that getting in with the popular and wealthy kids at school would be the best place to begin. Although she attended a public school, its boundaries had radically changed in the name of equality; they had changed to encompass Marisa's lower class neighborhood. Some of the social elite were not happy with this development, but the school districts were determined to integrate all of the schools with the reasoning that this would create a sense of equality. It was part of an era, the way it was. Marisa did not know or care why the boundaries were changed. She was just glad they were. If she had to cross over the freeway to get to school, she would do it.

Marisa developed a plan and started hanging out on the outskirts of the in-groups. The "Ins," simply would not allow the *new intruders* into their closed inner circles.

Marisa hoped for the day they would invite her *in*. She prayed, to one day be noticed. She believed in her heart that they would, one day, allow her into their elite clique. The day soon came while waiting in the lunch line.

Ethan was talking. "I'm going to be having my bar mitzvah soon, and I'm going to have the hottest party this town has ever seen. We're going to have the reception at the Saratoga Hills Country Club, and you're *all* invited."

Marisa had difficulty sitting through the rest of her afternoon classes. She could barely conceal her joy.

Marisa ran all the way home that day, shouting to her inner self, "At last! I'm in!" Joyfully, she told her mother all about the up and coming party.

Her mother, warmly and promisingly said she would, talk to her father about it – as soon as he arrived home. And she did.

"Charlie, Marisa has been invited to a party at the Saratoga Hills Country Club," Cassie said as she handed him a beer.

He took a deep swig. "Well ... She's not going."

"I know we don't have the money to go out and buy her a dress. But I could sew her one."

"It's not the money. You know that ..."

"I understand your concerns, Charlie, I really do, but if you could have seen the look on her face when she came home today." She paused and smiled. "There was a glow to her that I haven't seen in a very long time."

Charlie set his beer down and approached his wife, the love of his life. "Okay, Sweetheart." He kissed her on her cheek, "I'll talk to her." How could he say no to either his soul mate or his precious daughter.

Charlie found Marisa flipping through the pages of an old and tattered society magazine. Ever since she went to work with him on *that day*, she would sit with her magazines and browse endlessly through its worn pages, staring at the Paparazzi photos in an absentminded daze.

"Daddy, this is what I want to look like when I grow up." Marisa showed him a page from her magazine. It was a photo of a beautiful woman, one that was standing in a lush garden with tall colorful flowers enveloping her. She wore a long blue satin dress and had a diamond and pearl necklace wrapped around her neck, one that seemed to sparkle, just like Marisa's eyes.

Oh boy, Charlie thought, he could tell the minute he saw her looking at the magazine that her going to any society party was definitely a bad idea. Charlie and Cassie had raised their kids to be free and to not adhere to any societal standards. He could tell by the far-away look in his daughter's eyes that she now wanted more. More than he had ever dreamed.

"Darling, I'm afraid we have to talk."

"Yeah?"

"Your mother told me about the party and I don't think it's such a good idea."

Tears welled up in Marisa's eyes. "Why not?"

"It's just not. That's all …"

"Daddy. Please. These kids don't even usually talk to me."

Charlie and Marisa came to an agreement, she would go to the party, and Cassie would make a dress for her.

Two months later on the night of *the party*, Marisa put on her beautiful new, blue satin-like dress. She picked white daises from their backyard and placed them in her hair with bobby pins. Her mother let her use her faux pearls.

"Tonight, I am going to be one of them." Marisa said under her breath as she got into her father's truck for the drive up to Saratoga Hills Country Club. Soon Marisa began to feel car sick, as they drove up the long winding mountain road, the road that led up to the exclusive "Members Only" club. She opened the truck's window and gasped for air, all the while trying not to let the wind mess her hair, her beautiful hair with the daisies pinned in it.

They passed through the gate and followed the signs leading up to the clubhouse. They had not spoken since they left home.

Horrified at the thought that anyone would see their old truck, Marisa pleaded with her dad to be dropped off while they were still a ways off and she started to open the door to get out.

"Marisa, close that door before you get hurt. I'll drop you off in front."

"I'm just excited, that's all."

A man in a red vest and matching bow tie came over and opened the truck door for Marisa. She did not see the disapproving look he gave her.

"Have fun. I'll pick you up at eleven."

"Okay. Love you, Dad."

"Love you, too."

Marisa watched her father's truck as it drove away. She took a deep breath, turned, and looked at the country club, the palace that she was about to enter. It was her new world and her new life. It was her dream and she was about to start living it.

She took a moment to breathe in the jasmine that wafted in the air and marvel at the beauty of the valley that sprawled out below.

The lights of the city were starting to flicker on. She had heard in the local news that this breath-taking valley was now being called Silicon Valley. She didn't know exactly what that meant, but she knew one thing, she wanted this town and this valley to be hers.

The noise of other guests arriving brought her back to reality. Gina Maxwell was screeching with laughter and confidently leading a group of girls through the main door passing a man standing in the entrance way.

Marisa took a deep breath and started to follow them. She was finally on her way - into a beautiful, exciting new world.

The man abruptly stopped her. "And what is your name?"

"Oh, umm … Marisa. Marisa Taft."

"Let me see," he glanced through the invitation list. I don't have your name on my list."

"But I was invited!"

"Do you happen to have your invitation with you?"

"Well … No." She knew she hadn't received a written invitation but she knew she'd been invited. "Ethan said everyone was invited."

"Wait here, I'll be right back." He hated these kid parties. The brats all thought they owned the place.

Marisa thought about sneaking in, but the man's demeanor had made her nervous and she didn't want to make a scene.

A few minutes passed. From the doorway where she stood, she could see into the ballroom. The room was decorated with balloons and flowers and a long banquet table shimmered with crystal glasses; silver serving trays were heaped with delicious looking food. Tall candles placed along the length of the tables gave the whole scene an ethereal glow and large floral arrangements on tables filled with food.

"There's a girl here who says she's invited but her name is not on the list."

"Oh, let her in for goodness sake." Mrs. Bernstein said then taking a sip from her champagne cocktail.

"Okay, I just wanted to check with you and Dr. Bernstein."

"That's fine." Dr. Bernstein said. "By the way, what is her name?"

"Marisa something. Taft, I think."

"Did you say Taft?"

"Yes. That's right. Taft."

Dr. Bernstein face turned ashen. Taft was an unusual name. What were the odds of the girl being from that family? No, he was not a gambling man. "Wait. On second thought, she's not to be let in."

"What are you talking about darling," Mrs. Bernstein said.

"I have my reasons …"

The bouncer was surprised at Dr. Bernstein's reaction but he was not paid to make judgments, he was paid to keep these people happy, and if it meant turning away a little girl, then he'd do what he was told.

"They said they've never heard of you. I checked with Ethan himself," he lied. "You understand. I don't make the rules, I just follow them, and I can't let you in."

What was he talking about?

"No, you're wrong. I was invited."

"Well you don't have an invitation now do you?"

There had to have been some terrible mistake. She was invited. She knew that she had never received a written invitation in the mail ... *But, that day at school. That day when Ethan invited everyone ...*

The realization of what was happening sunk in and Marisa's thoughts turned sour. How could she have been such a fool? She was just an outsider, someone who stood around waiting and wanting to belong, always at the edge of the crowd and never really a part of it.

They would never accept her into their world. She would never be able to tell her father the ugly, truth. She couldn't bring herself to call her father, to ask him to come and get her. She would just have to wait until the night was over. She would never belong, not as part of this world.

She shivered as she caught glimpses of the social interaction inside through a window – *always through a window ...*

Some people were coming out onto the patio to get some fresh air or more likely to seek some privacy for some more serious romance. Trying to make herself invisible, she prayed no one would see her – it was too late to try and run now. Then her worst fears became reality as the mocking laughter of Gina Maxwell, the snobbiest girl of them all, spotted her in the bushes.

Unable to move, Marisa stayed where she was; she was paralyzed with fear and humiliation. She felt trapped like a wild animal so expecting the worst she got down on the ground and tried to curl up to make herself smaller and shut her eyes tight. To her relief and surprise, nothing happened ... Gina apparently had decided, for whatever reason, to avoid a scene at that moment. Besides Gina was too busy flirting with a guy she was trying to impress.

Well, there was no hurry, Gina thought. She would store this little tidbit of information for future use. What a laugh! Imagine Marisa Taft trying to crash this party. What nerve!

The night was passing at a crawl. Marisa wondered how much time had passed and how much longer she would have to endure the cold before her father would arrive in his noisy old truck. She tried in vain to convince herself that she would be fine.

Joshua, one of Ethan's invites from another school, went outside to get some fresh air. The live band music blasting from inside the club distracted him from his thoughts. His parent's recent divorce had left him feeling like a pawn. They insisted he attend this party, for a kid he didn't even know. After the divorce, they moved to Santa Rosa but his mother kept contact with her socialite friends. She was such a wanna-be, always trying to get him to fit in with kids he wanted no part of.

He leaned down to pick up a flower, a daisy -- a white daisy. He glanced up and saw the most beautiful girl he had ever seen. She appeared to him like some kind of nymph rising magically out into the moonlight.

"Who are you and what on earth are you doing out here?"

Marisa almost burst into tears, but held them back so she wouldn't make a fool of herself in front of this handsome guy.

They took turns listening and talking, feeling an instant bond; able to share things they had never been able to share with anyone. She told him how she felt as if she had been born into the wrong family and into the wrong side of life. She told him how she had this fantasy of being queen of Silicon Valley and how she longed to be a part of a different world other than her own.

Joshua held her close and gave Marisa a tender kiss – her first kiss. A thrill went through her – she had never felt this way before. The roar of her father's old truck broke the quiet – an unwelcome intrusion forbidding her feelings. She knew she must go.

"Wait!" He yelled after her, "What's your name?"

"Marisa. Marisa Taft ... from the wrong side of the tracks ... the wrong side of life!"

He laughed and yelled back, "My name is Josh. Joshua McKenzie!"

But that was then, and she'd never forget the humiliation of that night, and how Joshua made her sorrows disappear with a simple kiss.

Chapter Five

Marisa, finally woke from her thoughts of the past, got up and almost finished packing. It was coming along nicely until she went into her bathroom, where once she had been proud when it had been featured in *Bed & Bath*, but now it only made her feel weary. Looking at her reflection she felt too tired to go on. She felt like going back to bed, maybe forever. What was the rush now anyway? Besides her girls, anyone who meant anything to her, were now dead.

As she crawled back into bed, she pushed aside the blue flannel blanket and reached for the shawl. It seemed like such a little thing in her life, right then, yet it gave her a moment of comfort.

Letting her mind drift back to when she was fourteen – was that when it all began? She had tried so hard to put it all behind her that now it was like opening wounds that were healed over. Had they ever really been healed or was it only on the surface? As she lay there, she remembered how it was, that bleak day in November.

Leaves had fallen to the ground and left the trees bare and lifeless. A chill filled the air and the clouds were dark and filled with rain waiting to burst forth.

"Mom, don't you have to get going?"

Cassie lay on the couch unable to find the willpower to get up and get ready to go to her job. Her body refused to move in spite of the nagging need for money that kept nudging and needling her. She drifted in and out of sleep until finally, her fatigue won out and she let herself be swallowed up in it.

Drifting in and out of sleep, she cursed herself for agreeing to help at Mrs. Greenville's tea.

Mrs. Greenville's daughter was scheduled to make her presentation into society along with nine other girls in her group. Not just anyone could join. One had to be chosen, or nominated, by someone that was already elected into the program. Written recommendations, as well as a formal interview of mother and daughter were rigid requirements.

Once chosen, the real work began. The mothers and daughters would spend years in preparation for the day that their daughter was ready to be presented.

It would all take place at a formal ball that would be a major extravaganza. Nothing was spared to make these galas the most spectacular and glitzy event of the year. Not to make the guest list could completely ruin one's social standing and status.

Cassie Taft did not have time for gossip and teas. She was too busy serving the women that did. Except for one cloudy day in November when she simply could not do it anymore.

Marisa looked down at her mother. Her long auburn hair, which she usually wore in a bun, fell loose and free around her face. Her face was pale -- almost translucent. Her hands were folded and rested upon her stomach.

Marisa noticed then, for the first time, that her mother had lost a lot of weight. And she saw the dark circles that had formed under her mother's once beautiful eyes. She looked at her mother differently – for the first time. She held her mother's hand and prayed. "Please God ..."

Marisa went to her bedroom and removed a shawl from her bed. Her mother had spent many hours knitting the shawl for her, her only gift that Christmas. She had been disappointed, hoping for something more glamorous, but later she had begun to appreciate it and sought its comfort. Now she placed it tenderly around her mother's thin body, wishing there was something more she could do.

Making a decision, she knew that there was something she could do and she knew what it was. She kissed her mother and told her father she was going out.

On her way out the door, she took change from her mother's purse for the bus ride and an umbrella because it looked like rain.

When Marisa arrived at the Greenville estate an hour later, she approached the house with uneasiness. She rang the front door bell. No answer. She rang it again, still no answer. Finally, on third ring, Mrs. Greenville came to the door.

"Yes, dear?" Mrs. Greenville said. "Who are you? Aren't you the servant's daughter? Where's your mother, parking the car?"

"My mother's at home."

"Oh? I hadn't noticed, oh yes, she's supposed to be helping in the kitchen."

"Well, I'm Marisa. My mother isn't feeling well, so I thought if I could work on her behalf?"

"Yes, how nice, but you need to enter the house through the service entrance, around back."

Marisa went around the side of the house and down the long driveway. She passed a man wearing a chauffeur's cap and said hello to him as she opened and entered the house through the back door marked, SERVICE ENTRANCE.

The door entered into a huge kitchen. On the kitchen counter where silver trays filled with small sandwiches with their crusts cut off. Marisa peeked inside one of the sandwiches. She discovered, to her surprise, that they were filled with cucumbers.

"Marisa, what are you doing?" Mrs. Greenville asked. "If you're going to take the place of your mother you need to change."

Directing Marisa to a bathroom that was through a pantry filled with more food than Marisa had ever seen. Marisa paused and looked at all the food, cans, boxes, and bags -- enough for months. Marisa didn't know that people kept that much food in their home. Suddenly, she remembered that she hadn't eaten.

Marisa looked in the bathroom. The bathroom was not like she imagined a bathroom to look like in a house as big as the Greenville's. It was white and sterile looking. There was a hand written note taped to the mirror. HIRED HELP – WASH YOUR HANDS.

On one wall of the bathroom was a black short-sleeved polyester dress, hanging on a bent metal hanger. Attached to the dress was a white cotton apron. "Oh, my God." She hoped Mrs. Greenville wasn't expecting her to wear the maid's black and white uniform. Confused, she walked back into the Greenville kitchen. Mrs. Greenville was in a fury. "Ramón, I told you to park the Bentley into the garage."

Marisa stood at the end of the kitchen counter, waiting for Mrs. Greenville to calm down. Marisa looked around the huge kitchen and visualized her mother down on her knees scrubbing the floor. Mrs. Greenville broke into her train of thought.

"What are you waiting for? My guests will be arriving soon."

Mrs. Greenville walked over to the bathroom and handed the servant's uniform to Marisa. "Put this on."

Slipping into the dreaded uniform she could not bring herself to even glance in the mirror but instead, vowed to be strong – she would get through somehow.

On entering the party room, the first person she saw was Gina Maxwell. And Gina made sure of that. "I'll have more tea, *Miss* Taft."

Marisa's humiliation was complete. "Oh God," she thought. "I don't know if I can do this!" But she was here now, and what did it really matter. The picture of her mother came flooding back dissolving the urge to give up and leave.

As Marisa was pouring the tea, Gina leaned in toward her and whispered. "I told everyone at Ethan's party about you hiding in the bushes. We laughed our asses off."

Marisa mouthed a "shut up."

"What did you say?"

"Nothing, I said nothing."

Marisa thought about simply throwing the hot tea to the floor or better yet on Gina's face. Instead, she went into the kitchen and held back the tears she knew would be forthcoming.

"Marisa, take this platter out."

Glancing at Mrs. Greenville, she wondered who was the bigger bitch, Mrs. Greenville or Gina.

Marisa lifted the heavy silver tray and it slipped from her hands and clattered to the floor scattering little sandwiches all over the tiles.

"Shit" Marissa said under her breath.

"I'll have no language like that in *my* house!" Mrs. Greenville spit out.

"It was an accident."

As Marissa squatted down to pick up the spilled sandwiches and tray, Mrs. Greenville leaned down and squeezed Marisa's arm. "Clean this up and get back to work."

Marisa stifled her tears as she thought about all of the humiliation her mother had probably suffered, and yet she had never complained.

In her mind, to get through this day, she created a fantasy. She was the daughter of a wealthy landowner, and she was assisting her overworked servants.

When the tea was over, Marisa changed back into her clothes. Her imagination got her through the ordeal and now she was free to leave. She threw the demeaning outfit on the floor of the bathroom and ripped up the note taped to the mirror reminding the *Help* to wash their hands. She grabbed the envelope Mrs. Greenville left on the kitchen counter for her, containing cash for her day's work, and fled out the front door. She vowed to never use a servant's door – ever again.

Chapter Six

Marisa tried to make the haunting memories of that day disappear. She pulled the shawl up over her head as if doing so would change the past. She lay there with her eyes open and thought about when she was fifteen.

"Dad. I'm trying out for cheerleading."

"How much is this going to cost me?" Her father said in a teasing voice.

"Dad, is that all you ever think about is how much things cost?"

No, Charlie was only thinking about one thing, his wife Cassie. She hadn't been looking her usual self and she seemed very tired, actually pale.

"All I need is a uniform and shoes. The school will provide us with pompoms," Marisa said.

"Mari, you know we don't have money for frivolous things." Charlie wanted to concentrate on his daughter's desires for what she wanted but he couldn't think about that now.

And his daughter, Marisa, didn't know that he had other things on his mind, like his wife's health.

"It's not frivolous," Marisa insisted. Noticing the serious look on her father's face, she decided not to pursue her effort. "Never mind. Cheerleading is not important, it doesn't matter," Marisa lied.

The next day while Marisa was half-sleeping through Spanish class, the school nurse came into the room. The two huddled like they were talking about something top secret and then her teacher told Marisa that she was excused from class.

"What for?"

"Just go with Mrs. Browning to her office."

In what seemed like slow motion, they walked down the drafty school hallway to her office. Marisa trembled as thoughts raced through her head as to what the nurse wanted. Did she want to make sure her immunizations were current? Did she want Marisa to volunteer in the health center? There was a TV on in the office. Then Marisa realized what she wanted. It was about her brother in the war. He must be dead. Gasping for air she thought she would need the oxygen tank that was sitting in the corner of the room.

"I'm sorry to tell you this," the nurse began slowly, "but your—your, mother has taken ill. She's been taken to the hospital and your father wants you to go there right away."

"My mother?"

She had just enough change for the bus ride to the hospital. She entered at the emergency room entrance where the flashing lights of an arriving ambulance guided her. Once inside, she looked for her father.

She went up to a desk marked CHECK IN. She was told to go to the third floor. Walking over to a desk with a sign on it that read ONCOLOGY UNIT, Marisa felt her legs weaken.

"Excuse me. I'm Marisa Taft. I'm looking for my mother."

"Cassandra Taft? She is in room 301. Down the hall and to your right."

With apprehension and fear, Marisa peered into the hospital room. She was startled to see her mother lying there. She didn't look like the person she hugged and kissed goodnight the evening before. How could she change so quickly?

Her father started to cry when Marisa quietly entered the room.

"I'm so glad to see you," he said.

"What's going on? Is mother going to be okay?"

"I'm going to be straight with you, she's very ill."

"I don't understand."

"Mother collapsed while she was at the Greenville's house, cleaning."

"What was that bitch making mother do?"

"No. No. It wasn't like that. She just collapsed. Then Mrs. Greenville called an ambulance."

"Wasn't that kind of her!"

Charlie ignored her remark.

"The doctor said she is in the advanced stages of ovarian cancer."

"I still don't understand. She seemed fine when I saw her last night." But Marisa had known in her heart that her mother was not fine.

Leaning over the hospital bed, she kissed her mother on her pale cheek. Her mother forced her lips into a half smile.

Her father said, "Mari, sit down."

"I'd rather stand."

"The doctor explained that your mother's cancer has already spread to other parts of her body."

"Well, when will she be getting out?"

"Soon."

"How will they treat it? When will she be back to normal?"

"I'm sorry honey, I'm afraid it's too far along."

"There must something they can do!"

"Precious, at this point, there's no hope ..."

Marisa felt the blood drain from her face and fainted. When she came to, she thought she was having a dream -- a nightmare. Only when she opened her eyes did she realize it was all too real. She hugged her mother, cried, and would not let go.

Cassandra Taft lived for another three weeks before she passed away at home in her sleep, surrounded by her loving husband and daughter.

As Charlie was making a series of phone calls and he knew there was one more call to make. With hesitation, he dialed the number he got from his wife's address book.

"Hello?"

"This is Charlie. Charlie Taft."

"What do *you* want?"

"I have some bad news. It's about Cassie ... Cassandra."

There was no response and Charlie thought maybe the line went dead. "You there?"

"Yes, I'm here!" His voice was filled with anger as hearing Charlie's voice reminded him of the pain Charlie had brought his family.

"I'm sorry to have to tell you this but Cassie is dead."

Choking back his tears, Charlie wanted to tell him what he really thought of him, but this was not the time. He continued. "The funeral is Wednesday at eleven, it'll be at the ..." Before he could finish, he heard a dial tone.

Without her son or parents present, Cassandra was laid to rest on a warm winter day in the local Catholic cemetery.

Marisa dressed in a navy blue dress with black flat shoes and wore her mother's string of pearls.

"You look just like your mother ..."

But that wasn't what Marisa wanted to hear from her father, not now, not at this point in time If he wanted to make her feel better, he failed miserably. She wanted her mother, not a comparison.

Marisa sat through the funeral mass with a benevolent grace, never once shedding a tear. Before the pallbearers removed the casket from the church, Marisa leaned over and kissed the wooden coffin - one last kiss for her mom.

When they arrived at the cemetery, a row of folding chairs surrounded the gravesite with one chair empty in a symbolic gesture for her brother, Johnny's absence.

Marisa and her father sat next to each other and held hands throughout the service. After the last prayer was read, a stoic Marisa stood up and tossed, one by one, white daises, ones her mother had grown in their own backyard, onto the pine casket as it was lowered into the cavernous hole in the ground.

Chapter Seven

Marisa spent the high school football season watching the games from the bleachers. She'd go to the last row, up high, where no one could see or talk to her. She didn't want to answer inquisitive questions about her brother away at war or her mother dying.

As she watched the cheerleaders down below, she tried not to think about her mother. She tried not to think about her brother. She watched the cheerleaders with envy, especially Gina Maxwell, who she watched with deep hostility.

Gina and the other cheerleaders wore their new outfits, short royal blue skirts, and matching blue and gold sweaters, with pride. The expensive cheerleading outfits were what made the difference of Marisa leading a cheer or having to listen painfully as the girls giggled their way through them.

Not having the money for an outfit kept her off the team, but she still had her pride. She'd still show her school spirit by going to the games, besides it was better than being bored at home. Home was too lonely and simply too painful. Her father did his best to cheer her up but her sadness remained deep inside her heart.

Clyde Tripp was one of Marisa's only friend's and tried his best to cheer her up. He sat with her in the bleachers. He wasn't cute or popular. Didn't play sports. And he had this bad habit of picking at the acne on his face. But he had become a loyal and trusted friend who asked for nothing of her in return for allowing him to just be with her. After all, they were alike in their aloneness – in always being on the fringes – not ever being part of the group. He had a brother that worked in a liquor store that was the same age as Johnathan but his brother had been excused from the draft because of a heart murmur.

Clyde searched in his mind for some way to bring a smile to Marisa's lips. He wasn't sure why she seemed so sad most of the time. Whether it was because she grieved for the loss of her mother or fears about

Johnathan in Viet Nam or maybe because she was not on the cheerleading team or most likely for all of those reasons. He just knew he had to do something. Suddenly he had an idea. "Marisa, come with me to the party after the game!"

Marisa was gazing down at the football field, feigning an interest she did not really feel.

"Touch down!" She heard in the distance.

"Marisa, listen to me for a minute. I've been invited to Gina's after the game."

She heard Clyde talking but she wasn't listening. Her thoughts were elsewhere.

"We're all meeting there after the game."

Turning to him, his face radiated. "What did you say?" She asked.

"Come with me to the party."

Clyde spoke almost like he fit in. "I don't know … where is it?"

"In the Rosegarden. I hear it's a huge house and best of all – no parents, they're out of town."

"Really? That sounds fantastic. Of course I'll go!"

Clyde quit picking at his skin and spent the rest of the game beaming.

When the game was over, Marisa called her father. "Someone is having a party and I just wanted to call you to let you know that I'll be home late tonight."

"Okay honey, thanks for letting me know. Call if you need a ride home."

"I will."

Marisa got into the car with Clyde. The driver was Jeffrey Torn, but everyone just called him by his initials, J.T. He had a black 1969 Camaro with a 350 engine. Marisa didn't know about cars but was hearing all about them on the drive. Soon J.T. pulled a handful of red pills out of his pocket. "Just a head start on the partying," he said, smiling. He swallowed one and gave one to Marisa another to Clyde who both followed suit.

The Camaro turned into the back parking lot of the liquor store, and Clyde got out and walked toward the building.

Marisa asked, "Are we going to be here long?"

J.T. turned around and glared at her. "Just mind your own business!"

J.T.'s demeanor had taken a sudden turn for the worse. Suddenly things were becoming ugly. A cold shiver of fear and panic ran through Marisa – she wished she had not been so trusting, swallowing that pill.

Clyde knocked on a windowless steel door where his brother would be able to let him in. There was a security camera in the front of the store, but not in the back. They could get away with lifting some liquor there, without anyone being wiser.

"And don't forget the whiskey," J.T. yelled out the car window, "and get the good kind, not that shit you usually get."

Clyde stood at the door waiting. Finally, in what seemed like an eternity to Marisa, the door opened and Clyde disappeared inside. She tried to stop shaking but her heart was pounding and she was beginning to feel strange – like she was floating somewhere and just an observer – not in control. She glanced over at J.T. who had just lit a cigarette.

"Do you have to smoke?"

"What's it to you?"

"It's just that the smoke makes me sick."

"Get out of the car if you don't like it."

Rolling down the car window of the backseat, Marisa tried to get some fresh air then spent the rest of the time waiting for Clyde, in silence.

Holding a bag filled with liquor bottles, Clyde returned and they drove off with the sound of squealing tires and blue smoke from burning rubber.

The party was in the affluent Rosegarden area of San Jose. Marisa knew the neighborhood well, but only from the outside. When she didn't take the bus to school, she'd walk by the palatial homes to and from school.

J.T. pulled his car into the driveway as if he owned the place. Marisa got out of the car, feeling woozy. "So, this is Steven's house?"

J.T. glared at her. "Steven? No, this is Gina's pad."

"Gina … Gina Maxwell?"

"The one and only."

Marisa felt a pit in her stomach. "Take me home."

"No way." J.T. had a disgusted look on his face.

"Clyde, you didn't tell me the party was at Gina's house!"

"Yes, I did. You just weren't listening. Come on Marisa," he said taking her hand. "It'll be fun." He guided her up the brick pathway leading to the two-story Colonial house.

She never would have anything to do with Gina but she needed to get some water or something, anything to make her feel better, even if it meant entering the witch's house for a few minutes.

The house was filled with people, and Marisa made her way to the kitchen. "Well, well, well. Look who's here," Gina said, her eyes burning into Marisa's.

"I'm not staying," Marisa blurted out. "I just wanted a glass of water."

"Hell, stay as long as you like."

"That's okay."

"Miss Taft, you look a little pale."

Marisa ignored the *Miss Taft* remark. "I don't feel so good."

"You probably just need something to eat. Here, try one of these brownies. I made them myself."

Marisa heard the words come out of Gina's mouth but it was as if she was speaking in monotone. She ate the brownie, washing it down with water and slumped down into the nearest chair, hoping the little bit of food would stop her dizziness.

"Hey, let's go dance," Clyde said, entering the kitchen.

"I don't think I can get up."

"Of course you can."

He led her into the backyard where the blaring music only added to Marisa's growing headache.

"Don't just stand there, dance!"

"I can't Clyde. That brownie is making me feel weird."

"You didn't eat one of Gina's brownies, did you?"

"Yeah, why … she poison it or something?

"Jesus, Marisa, I can't leave you alone for a minute. She did do *something* ... those brownies are laced with marijuana."

"Oh God Clyde," Marisa said as she teetered near the edge of the swimming pool. Then someone nudged Marisa from behind and pushed her in. She couldn't breath as the shock knocked the wind out of her.

"What did you do that for?" Clyde said as he shoved Gina causing her to fall to the concrete.

"You stupid fool. Get out of my house!"

"Oh believe me, we will."

Clyde jumped into the pool, grabbing Marisa as she struggled to catch her breath.

Gina got up from the ground as people around her were laughing. She didn't care about that, but her taunting of Marisa was not over. "Oh, did poor Miss Taft want to go for a swim? I would have lent you one of my many suits ..."

"Gina, you are such a slut," Clyde said.

Clyde helped Marisa out of the pool and told J.T. he needed to borrow his car to take Marisa home.

"Fine," he said sarcastically. "But don't be long. And don't rev the engine!"

Clyde helped Marisa to her front door. "I'll be fine now," Marisa said as she hugged Clyde.

"Night baby doll." He kissed her on her cheek and returned to the party, just long enough to toss J.T. his keys back.

Marisa's body craved sleep but inside her head, her mind kept racing around bombarding her with words and thoughts that she did not want to listen to. When she tried to will herself to shut them out, she had the feeling that someone was in the room, shaking her. She was sure that she heard her mother's voice. She was certain she felt her mother's cool hand upon her forehead.

Suddenly, she knew. *Johnny was home!* Her mother was trying to tell her Johnny was home!

Marisa was filled with gratitude as she realized she was not having a dream – her brother was finally back from the devastating war.

Her prayers had been answered – how intensely she had prayed with her mother pleading for Johnny's safety and that he would come home to stay. It had been a shock to the family when Johnny was drafted – he had had no plans to be in the Military but had accepted the call when it came without protest even though he was against the war in principle. He wore the uniform with pride and determined to make the best of it.

Watching the news every night, the Taft family was always horrified by the pictures they saw of villages being blown apart; innocent women and children running trying to escape into the jungle, scenes that were of a different kind of war than what they had ever imagined war to be.

They heard no word from Johnny. At least they had not received a telegram saying, "We regret to inform you that ..."

Leaning down she gave a sleeping Johnathan a peck on his tanned cheek. His black combat boots stood open-laced in the corner of the room, his green camouflaged army jacket rested nearby. Printed in black letters, on the front pocket, was one word, TAFT.

She could not wait any longer for this moment so she shook him until he woke up out of his deep slumber.

For the next two weeks, Johnny picked Marisa up every day after school. They drove around for hours, talking and laughing at the world. She could talk and he intently listened. She told him all about school, about not being able to be a cheerleader, and about her only friend Clyde, and they laughed. Then her brother would turn serious and tell her of his ventures into the jungles of Viet

Nam, what the war was really like, about all the people dying and about losing friends in battle.

The pain of losing their mother was less severe with the sibling bond they shared. And then it was over. The knock on the front door came in the middle of a foggy bay area night. Killed by a hit and run driver, *Johnny was dead.*

Chapter Eight

Marisa continued the pretense of living a somewhat normal life, yet inside, she was drowning in grief. How she treasured those few weeks after Johnny came back from war, then tucked away her memories along with the flowers she had dried and pressed from his casket – unable to look too closely at any of it.

What cruel twist of fate would bring him home through the war unharmed only to suddenly steal his life in such an insane way?

The remainder of Marisa's high school years -- were but a blur in her memory. After graduation, she enrolled in the local community college. On days when she wasn't studying or working in her part-time job at the movie theatre, she would borrow her father's truck and drive over the hill to the beach. Sometimes, she would stop mid-way up the hill, at Castle Rock, and stare down at the valley. Castle Rock was a giant rock that you could climb on and see the entire valley floor. She would sit for hours and try not to think about how lonely she felt. About how much she missed her beloved mother and brother.

She saw Clyde on occasion. He worked at a gas station, where he would give Marisa free gas. In return, she would give him a quick kiss on his pockmarked scarred face.

She signed up for computer programming classes and learned all she could about interfacing and CPU's. If she were going to be a presence in the Valley, she would need to learn about these things and how they operated.

One day, in computer class, someone handed her a flyer for a party that was being thrown by a fraternity at Santa Rita University. Santa Rita was the local private university, recognized for providing talent to the Silicon Valley companies.

She stuck the flyer in her backpack. She was going to have a busy night. She had a homework assignment, which was more important than going to a party.

Her father had gone out for the evening and the house was quiet and still. Marisa spread her notebooks across the kitchen table and began her studies. Her homework assignment was to come up with an idea for a business model. She had an idea that had been floating around in her head for weeks but formulating it on paper was something else.

Marisa's mind began to wander almost as quickly as she started to work. She scribbled a series of zzz's, and then wrote, "what next?" as if the simple task of writing words on a piece of paper would provide an answer.

Trying to think of a name for her on-paper company, she made different combinations of the letters as if she were playing a game of scrabble. She toyed around, trying out different names until she came up with the name of Zanex.

Then she glanced around the kitchen and couldn't help but think of her mother. She envisioned her mother baking some oatmeal cookies and pouring her a glass of milk. Tears welled up in her eyes.

She rose and poured herself a glass of water. She couldn't concentrate. She opened the kitchen window to let some air in but even the cool evening air didn't help much. She turned on the radio, which was tuned to a classical station, which only made her sleepy. She had to get out of the house.

She went to the hall closet, pulled out Johnny's army jacket, and put it on. It gave her comfort but at the same time sent a sharp pang through her chest as the familiar scent enveloped her.

She went into her father's bedroom. All of her mother's things were still there. Her clothes, her costume jewelry, and even her perfume still seemed to linger about the room. She felt a wave of nausea and went into the bathroom and began searching through the medicine cabinet. She pulled out a bottle of tranquilizer pills that had been prescribed to her father after her mother's death. Without giving it a second thought, she put the pill bottle into the pocket of Johnny's jacket.

She returned to the kitchen, turned off the radio, and fumbled with her class notes but she was having a hard time concentrating.

She filled a glass with whiskey. She took one sip, then another, and yet another. Then she called Clyde. "Hey, what's going on?"

"Not much."

"You want to go to a party?"

"Yeah, sounds good, where is it at?"

"Near the university."

"Which one?"

"Santa Rita."

"Give me ten minutes and I'll pick you up."

Clyde and Marisa wound their way through the streets surrounding the university. Looking for a residence that the flyer simply described as the "blue house." They soon found it by following the steady stream of cars and pedestrians.

A guy stationed at the front door announced to them that it was five dollars each to come in. Marisa and Clyde looked at each other with the same question in mind.

"Do you have any cash?"

"No, do you?"

"No, but I do have an idea," Clyde said grabbing Marisa's hand. "Follow me." He led her to the side yard fence, which they climbed over, getting in for free.

The fraternity house was packed with wall-to-wall people. Some dancing, some making-out, others already passed out. Glancing around, she saw some cute guys but she thought that they were making fools of themselves by being so inebriated. Jealously filled her as she looked at a group of girls, probably sorority sisters. They were dressed to the nines and looked flawless -- even drunk.

A sudden curiosity came over her as to why she even wanted to come to this party. She wasn't smart like these kids, didn't have the money, clothes or cars they did. Didn't have a trust fund, ski cabin, beach house, or rich grandparents funding a prestigious university education. She never even knew her grandparents; they had passed away years before she was born.

As she glanced around the room, the air a mixture of pot and cigarette smoke, the kids in different stages of drunkenness or being stoned, she wondered why she felt so insecure. She wished she had the money to attend a high priced college like Santa Rita. For some reason not having material things or money made her feel like a lesser person.

Wedged between a beauty queen and a football type, Clyde was taking a drag on marijuana joint. "Clyde," she whispered. "Maybe we should get out of here."

"What are you talking about? You're the one that wanted to come to this party."

"I know, but I've changed my mind."

"Look, I didn't drive all the way out here just to turn around and leave. Besides there's some good weed floating around here. Can't you smell it?"

"Yeah, and it's making me sick."

"Honestly Marisa, you're such a wuss."

"Okay, fine, we'll stay for awhile, but help me find the bathroom quick."

"Jesus, you always have to go to the bathroom. Can't you find it yourself?"

"I had too much to drink earlier, that's all. Just help me maneuver through all these people, please."

"Fine," he said. He adored Marisa, but sometimes she could be a pain in the ass. But she was his platonic friend and they had a bond that went back to childhood.

Clyde and Marisa walked down the hallway passing by shut doors covered in posters advertising everything from Budweiser to hot babes in bikinis.

"Here's the bathroom," Clyde said in an assuming voice, as he opened the door.

Kneeling on the floor, next to a coffee table, a guy had his face lowered to a mirror. He snorted white powder up his nostril and then glanced up at Marisa. "Hello beautiful."

"I was -- just looking for the bathroom."

"Want a line?" He held a rolled up hundred dollar bill toward Marisa.

"Uhh … no, that's okay," Marisa turned around to walk out.

"I'll have some," Clyde said enthusiastically.

"Clyde!" Marisa was indignant.

"You are *no* fun," Clyde said to Marisa.

"Maybe later," Clyde said. "Thanks for the offer."

"Yeah, right,," the guy said as he passed the bill to the person next to him.

Clyde and Marisa turned the corner of the hallway, which led into yet another hallway.

"Jesus, this house is like a maze," Clyde said. "Next door on your right I bet it's the bathroom."

"How do you know?"

"Look at the people waiting outside the door."

"Oh, good assessment, but shit, I gotta go now!"

"Let us through," Clyde said, pushing his way to the front of the line. He wanted to get Marisa into the bathroom and then he could get back to the other lines … the cocaine ones …

"Thanks love," Marisa said before she shut the bathroom door.

"See you later," Clyde said, his voice trailing off.

In the bathroom, Marisa looked down at the filthy toilet and suddenly her urge to urinate vanished. The floor was cluttered with wads of tissue and Hustler magazines. Endless dripping from the faucet into the rust-stained sink was irritating to say the least. She wasn't sure what was worse, the Peter Frampton music blaring from the living room or the incessant drip … drip … drip.

Looking at her reflection in the water-stained mirror, she asked herself a question, "What am I doing here for God sakes?"

She had no answers. She only knew she felt a distinct feeling of aloneness. In a houseful of people, she never felt so lonely. She closed her eyes for a moment, ignoring the pounding on the door to "Hurry up in there," and tried to compose herself.

Reaching for the pill bottle inside the jacket pocket, an idea ran through her head that she should just swallow the pills. Would anyone care that she was gone? Anyone at all? Certainly not the people in this house.

She knew her father loved her but she felt she was a burden to him. He provided what he could as she worked her way through community college, but there never seemed to be enough money.

Her thoughts turned to her brother. She could not believe he was dead, killed by a hit and run driver. The thought of him surviving a horrendous war only to arrive home and then be run over by a car was incomprehensible.

"Hurry up," someone yelled, as they banged louder and louder on the locked bathroom door.

"Just a minute," Marisa said faintly, trying to hold back tears. The earlier whiskey had warmed her body but it still didn't take the anguish away.

With trembling hands she opened the plastic lid, shook some pills into the palm of her hand and told herself to just, "Do it, just do it. Do it and get it over with." Maybe next time around, she thought, she'd have a better life …

"You fall asleep in there?"

"I'll be right out." She quickly dropped the loose pills into her pocket and hurriedly left the bathroom.

"Well, it's about time," someone said.

"Have you seen Clyde?" She asked randomly.

"Don't know him."

"Never mind …"

Marisa went into the crowded kitchen and helped herself to a can of Pepsi. She heard someone say the keg in the backyard was empty and then a rush of people came into the house.

In the backyard, she found it to be in fact, void of people who were there earlier.

Marisa lay down on the grass. The evening fog hadn't rolled in yet and the stars were twinkling as if providing a night-light for the heavens above.

She played with the pills in her pocket, rolling them around her fingertips. She couldn't believe she'd been thinking of taking them and calling it a day. But then anger filled her body. Why had God taken away her mother, then her brother? One by one, her family was disappearing. Who would be next? What more pain had God in store for her? What more despair was waiting for her down the road? She decided not to wait around to find out.

Swallowing the pills would be the hard part ... dying easy.

The once brilliant stars faded as her vision blurred. The last thing she remembered was a dream she had when she was little, something about a kingdom and she was a queen, queen of something -- *Silicon something.*

Chapter Nine

One fraternity brother had enough fun for one evening. Parties tended to get out of control though he thought this one mild in comparison to others they had had, but he was tired of the whole college scene and wanted everyone to leave.

If his classmates wanted to make fools of themselves, he couldn't have cared less. He was the responsible one in the tribe. Having made friends with the campus police, they usually looked the other way when the frat house threw a party. He was known for being the organizer and keeper of order in an otherwise insane fraternity house.

He came to Santa Rita because of their business school and he wanted to be a part of the growing high-tech world, and it was a good place to start. First, he would clean up the crap, the party crap.

He started in the backyard. Empty beer cups and wine bottles lined the back porch. Cigarette ashtrays overflowed -- *slobs, all slobs.*

He dumped the garbage into a metal garbage can. Someone yelled from inside, "Be quiet out there you idiot!" He shook his head. He did one last check of the yard and noticed something or someone on the lawn.

Approaching the girl, she appeared lifeless.

"Oh my God!" This was the worst case of passing out he had ever seen. Lifting her up, he glanced down at her ashen face. For an instant he thought he'd met her before but all he could think about now was saving her life. Her body was limp as he placed her into the backseat. Why had no one noticed her lying there or missed her at the party? Who had she come with? He prayed it was not too late as he drove as fast as he dared to the hospital.

It was a long night as he waited for the doctors to pump her stomach and made sure she would be all right.

Charlie came rushing into the emergency room. The last time he was there was just before his wife died, and now after he received a call in the middle of the night, he prayed his daughter would live. He didn't know all the details, just that his daughter had been brought in with a possible overdose.

"I want to see my daughter," he said anxiously to the attendant at the ER desk.

"The doctors are still with her, and we'll let you know when you can see her. Just have a seat in the waiting room."

Charlie sat down and stared up at the TV in the corner of the room. How could anyone watch television at a time like this?

"Excuse me," a young man said approaching him. "Are you Marisa's father?"

"Yes, yes I am."

"I'm Josh. Joshua McKenzie. I was the one that brought her here."

Charlie demanded, "What the hell happened to my little girl? The doctors told me that she had overdosed on pills. Marisa would not take any kind of drugs. She would never do that ..."

"I don't know exactly what happened, but I found her in my backyard, she was passed out and I brought her here."

"What do you mean ... at your house?"

"The frat house. We were having a party."

"What kind of irresponsible, stupid thing were you doing?"

"I found a bottle, an empty bottle of tranquilizers. I gave the container to the doctor. I don't know how many she took …"

"Tranquilizers?"

"Yes sir, and I read the label, it had the name, Charlie Taft on it."

"Oh no!" Charlie's fury went from his daughter, from this young man, to himself. He should have thrown the pills away. He never took any, and now, his daughter could have died because of him.

"She's going to be fine. It was a close call, but she'll be fine."

Charlie lowered his head and covered his face with his hands. "If anything ever happened to her, I don't know what I'd do."

The two men waited a long night, not speaking but mindlessly watching the television set.

In the morning, Joshua went into the hospital gift shop where he bought some flowers. He had remembered during the lengthy wait where he had met her before. How could he ever forget? He was waiting for her when she was released. He was grateful he found her in time to be saved, and grateful that God had mysteriously brought her back into his life. When she was brought out of the emergency room, he and her father were waiting in anticipation to see her.

"Marisa, thank God you're fine." Her father embraced her. "You gave me a real scare. It would break my heart if anything happened to you."

"I know Dad, I'm sorry."

The fraternity brother greeted her with a broad smile as he asked her if she remembered him from long ago.

"Of course I do," she said.

"I'm so glad you're all right, and I'm so glad to see you again."

Marisa had tears of joy in her eyes as she looked into his eyes. Perhaps God was on her side after all ...

"Here, these are for you," Josh said, handing her a bouquet of daisies ... white daisies.

Chapter Ten

One Year Later

Marisa was planting an assortment of flowers, multi-colored petunias, red geraniums, and her favorites -- white daisies -- leading up the path to their front door.

The small house they rented in Fremont seemed to be perpetually in fog. The fog and its chilly moisture made her flowers bloom beautifully. She thought how she had once been in a fog, and how Joshua McKenzie saved her. Her flowers were representative of her new life -- the life saved by Joshua McKenzie.

Marisa and Josh married six months after they met. Marisa vaguely remembered him carrying her to the hospital. She remembered vividly that awful night when she had given up and swallowed those pills. Awful, but wonderful too, since that was the night Joshua had become her savior and soul mate.

Marisa Taft became Mrs. Joshua McKenzie. Marisa was proud to carry his name, the name of the man she loved. The man that saved her life, the man she fell in love with as a young teenager, and then came magically back into her life. Josh had made her a whole person again. He was her lifeline. He took her from a deep and consuming depression and gave her laughter and fun. He carried her into joyfulness, inner peace, and a renewal of her lost passion -- life itself.

After Ethan's party, Marisa thought she would never see Joshua, ever again but then he came into her life at the lowest point of her existence.

After they married, they moved to the East Bay where rent was inexpensive compared to the rest of the Bay Area. They didn't have much money, but they didn't need much.

Josh remembered the day he first met her, too. The day she stood outside the country club. The day he fell in love -- the day they both did.

After Josh graduated from college, he was hired by a start-up that sold a software program, one designed to increase business efficiency that they believed no other company was offering.

Very excited about their prospects and sure the new company was going to soar right to the top, they offered stock options as an incentive to recruit key people. Employees were expected to work sixteen-hour days and often were running on pure adrenaline and black coffee.

The start-up capital soon dwindled; promises of fresh money coming in seemed to evaporate. They hung on in desperation, not revealing their true financial state, hating to give up a dream that seemed so nearly within reach.

Just as suddenly as it all began, the bubble burst and the doors were closed. Josh was in shock to find himself among the unemployed – he probably could have seen the warning signs if only he had paid closer attention.

On the day that Josh went home with the news of his sudden unemployment, Marisa had some news for him too.

"I have something to tell you," she said as he walked into their living room. Marisa had adorned their dining room table with their best dishes, daises from her garden, and his favorite dinner of spaghetti and meatballs.

Josh loosened his tie as he sat down on the oak dining room chair. "It was a rough day," he said, putting his hand to his forehead like he had a headache. "I have something to tell you, too."

"You go first," Marisa said, subconsciously rubbing her belly.

"There were some cut backs at the office."

"Oh, that's too bad," Marisa said pouring him a glass of iced tea. "Anybody we know?"

"Yeah, a lot of people got laid off ... plus including me."

Marisa sat down, feeling dizzy.

"Did you say ... you got laid off?"

"That's right."

"For how long? When will you go back?"

"No, it's not like that. The company shut down. Everyone got fired."

"What are we going to do?" Marisa seriously asked.

Josh heaped a portion of spaghetti onto his plate. "We'll be fine ... don't worry about it. What was it you wanted to tell me?"

"This doesn't seem like the right time. This is not how I planned it," Marisa said shaking her head this way and that, "Not at all … not at all."

"Come on … just spit it out, what is it?"

"… I'm pregnant."

With a wide smile, Josh approached Marisa, gently touching her stomach, then put his arms around her to hug her. He was filled with mixed emotions -- both bliss and worry over how they would afford a baby with him being out of work. "This is great news," he said, "*Really* great news."

Marisa kissed him on the lips as Josh swept her off her feet and carried her to their bedroom where they made love. What better way of celebrating the fruit of their love, than by making love?

Several months went by and Joshua still had not found a job. They were down to their last thousand dollars and if he paid the house rent, then he would not be able to keep up their health insurance.

He decided to pay the insurance and if it came down to it, he could always ask for money from his mother and stepfather, not something he wanted to do, but he would.

"I'll be back this afternoon," Josh told Marisa as she put the morning dishes into the dishwasher. "Okay honey. Love you."

Marisa called her friend Linda. She had met Linda McGregor while attending classes at their local community college. Linda had given a talk to her English class about life as a journalist.

Linda began her career right from community college, before transferring to a state college. When she graduated, she was hired by the local metro newspaper to write their weekly society column. Linda was slowly but surely working her way up the journalistic ranks. She is also a ravishing good-looking redhead and at times had to convince her predominantly male co-workers to take her writing seriously. Someday, she would be off the gossip news and be covering more exciting stories than about who attended whose benefit.

Marisa and Linda struck up a friendship. They called or met for coffee every week. Linda lived in Saratoga, in a large house, sponsored not so much by her meager salary but by her husband, a player on the professional golf tour.

"Linda?" Marisa answered the phone.

"Good morning. Are you coming down for coffee this week?"

"I don't think so," Marisa said, her lips quivering as if she was in a freezing snowstorm.

"What's wrong? I can hear it in your voice."

Marisa and Linda talked about everything from sex to the best way to cook an artichoke, but one thing Marisa refrained from talking about, was money.

"How are you feeling?" Linda could tell Marisa was holding back. They were best friends and she knew when she was not being forthright.

"I'm fine. The babies are fine, too."

"Babies?" Linda laughed, "You mean there's more than one?"

"Twins. I'm having twins. But that wasn't what I was calling about."

"You mean there's more! What could be more exciting than bringing two babies into the world?"

The infectious good nature of Linda rubbed of on Marisa and she soon forgot about her money problems and prattled on about her babies.

"You know, Linda, I haven't told Josh yet -- that we're having twins. I mean, him being out of work and all. I don't want to stress him out more than he already has been. He's seems like a basket case and telling him would add to his burden"

"What? You have to tell him. Screw him being out of work. He has a responsibility to find anything he can to support you, but you have to tell him. Maybe this'll get his ass in gear!"

"Yeah, maybe you're right."

"Besides this is more important than money, I mean we're talking about two precious lives here ..."

Joshua walked into the Mission Church on the university campus. It was a Tuesday morning and the church was quiet. He sat in the last row of pews, rubbed his eyes and sighed. The church had special meaning for him in so many ways. Not only had he earned his college degree at Santa Rita, he and Marisa exchanged their wedding vows here in this very church. He thought his life was planned in the right direction and now it seemed to be crashing down all around him. He knelt down and prayed. "Please dear God, guide me ..."

Upon leaving the church, the fog had lifted and the sun was bright.

"Is that you Josh McKenzie?"

Turning around he saw his former Economics Professor.

"How are you doing young man?" The professor was holding a briefcase in one hand and a cup of coffee in the other.

"Professor Bolton, It's nice to see you. I'm fine. Just fine."

"Well, do you have a minute to catch up? I'd love to hear about what you've been up to since graduation."

"I've got all the time in the world."

"Let's sit down a minute." He motioned Joshua to sit on the bench in a garden area adjacent to the church.

"How's things going for you since graduation?"

"Well, as far as work is concerned, I've gone through a couple of start-ups. Joshua couldn't hide the downtrodden look on his face. "But right now, I'm sort of between jobs."

"How's that wife of yours?"

"Marisa? She's great. In fact, we're expecting our first child."

Professor Bolton put out his hand to shake Joshua's. "Congratulations," he said. "What a blessing."

"I guess it is."

"Of course it is my son. Family is the most important thing in life."

"Well, I've got to support my family," Josh said with a furrowed brow.

"You've been to the Career Center, right?"

"No, I didn't even think about it."

"Well, get your ass in gear and get over there."

Josh laughed. "I will. I will. By the way, where is it anyway?"

"How many years did you attend here?" Professor Bolton laughed. "It's in the University Center, across from the dining commons. Now I know you know where that is!"

Josh laughed. "I was just kidding!"

"Keep in touch. Okay Joshua?"

"Will do, and thanks Professor."

"Hey, you're an alumni now, call me Patrick!"

"Okay. It was great seeing you again, Patrick."

"Take care of yourself Joshua. Oh, and Josh?"

"Yes?"

"Remember it takes six or seven start-ups before you make your first million."

He laughed. "I'll remember that."

"So, as you can see," Joshua explained to the Career Counselor, "I'm in need of a job immediately."

"Today is your lucky day. There was a man in here this morning looking to hire bright young people such as you."

"That's fantastic. What's his name? What's the company? I'll give him a call right away."

"Here's his card. You might've heard of him, Mr. Lawson. Mr. Philip Lawson."

Chapter Eleven

Philip Lawson had become a force to be reckoned with in the software industry. He went from high school drop out to one of the top salesman at Orian, a successful database software company. His self-assured charm and good looks got him hired at Orian where he quickly moved up the ranks to become one of their top salespeople.

While at Orian, he learned everything he could and took that knowledge with him to start his own company.

His work at Orian proved quite beneficial to him, starting with their sales techniques. The salesmen sold products that didn't exist, at least not yet. The goal of any good software salesman was to get a sale first. They would sell the customer whatever the customer wanted to buy. They sold promises. They sold air -- Vaporware.

As one of Orian's top salesmen, his job was to get deals "signed." Once closed, Orian's software writers would first begin developing the purchased product. Eventually, the programmers would install their wares at the customer's site. Getting to that point wasn't his problem.

A major part of Philip's job was to propagate the never-ending sell cycle. Orian's salesmen became adept at selling their customers more software, and yet more software, to fix the software they had purchased in the first place. The circle was designed to never end. The software company grew rich, and their customers got screwed.

Philip would love to convince existing and potential new customers that what they really needed was the latest version, the latest release of their non-existent software.

The fact that the software didn't exist was never mentioned. He just sold them on the fact that they needed it. He wasn't lying, he just didn't tell them the whole truth. He didn't tell the customers that the programmers were still building the software and trying to work out the kinks. That was irrelevant to what he was doing. When the software was delivered, it was with a binder of unintelligible instructions that were impossible to understand. The customer then needed to hire consultants, provided by Orian, at exorbitant fees to train employees and implement the software that was sold to them in the first place.

When Philip wasn't selling, he was doing his boss, Brenda. He gave her sex, and in return, she gave him every top lead. They'd take long lunch breaks and always came back hungry.

Philip Lawson, with Brenda's help, was becoming the hottest wonder boy of Silicon Valley. The "Prince" he had been nicknamed by the local media. His goal was not only to live up to his reputation, but also to take home the coveted SilVa Award, the Valley's most prestigious recognized honor.

Philip spent his time listening and learning. He learned every trade secret, even little things, like how to sabotage his competition. He started doing juvenile

things, like when his customer's were up for a renewal
and the opposing competitors would come in to give
their latest product presentations, Philip knew there were
things he could do, to make his competitors look like
losers and he would look like a brilliant star.

He was known to have canceled his competitor's
car rental and hotel reservations. When the competing
company arrived, there would be no car available and
they'd have to hunt for a decent hotel room. He was just
learning at this stage, but he soon progressed to more
sophisticated forms of sabotage. All of this was done to
put Philip Lawson into a favored power position, and to
keep all others beneath him. He was in charge. He got the
deals. All was fair -- in the software wars of Silicon
Valley.

When Philip felt there was nothing left to learn at
Orian, he quit. Brenda threw a prolonged tantrum – until
he agreed he'd still see her on a *personal basis*.

When Philip left Orian, he insured his access to
the company mail system by creating a special password
and user ID code. He would continue to receive any
message that might prove helpful to him, and his new
company, Lawco.

He didn't care. He openly took notes and gathered
information on their ideas. He learned all about the

companies that Orian was trying to sign -- until he was caught. But by then, he had a formidable list of prospects and a multitude of ideas to operate with. His most valuable theft was the coveted key Customer Contact List and its projected new sales.

Philip eventually quit his snooping, but not until he had every key contact added to his own database.

Philip headed a short distance south to South Bay, the heart of Silicon Valley. He rented office space at a prime location on the corner of Scott and Bowers.

The next thing Philip did was to incorporate a name for his budding company. This was an effortless venture. He had been thinking about it for years. There was only one name flashing through his handsome head, Lawco -- after himself, of course.

Lawco Company would sell a new and improved version of the very same software that Orian sold.

At his newfound company, Philip trained all the salesmen himself. He taught them to, "Promise them anything!" And they did. Anything to get their deals signed. Philip took every little trick he learned while working with Brenda at Orian and applied it to Lawco. His underhanded business dealings were progressing to new levels. He had such magnetism and charisma that his customers simply could not say no to him.

He didn't care who he stepped on to get what he wanted because he knew -- to be a presence in the Valley it meant lying, and stealing prospects away from unsuspecting sales people from competing companies. He would just laugh after watching another company spend endless hours courting prospective customers, only to swoop in at the last minute and sign them with Lawco before the sales teams knew what hit them.

Philip was ruthless, cold, and cunning, yet always beautifully charming, as needed. This was Philip's management basis at Lawco. His employees had to fit his mold and his style or they wouldn't last more than a few weeks. Image, *his image*, was everything.

His key employees were hand picked, a team made to fit his every greed and still shine with an outwardly clean image. He snatched a few of his new staff from Orian. The rest he recruited from the outside.

He recruited graduates from the local prestigious Santa Rita University.

Arriving in Philip's office, Joshua showed up with resume in hand, a desire to work hard, and a want -- to learn from the master.

Philip hired him on the spot and Joshua became his number one protégé and team member of Lawco Software, a fast growing competitor.

Philip trained his new employees his way. He was the team leader, the Captain of his corporate ship. He would tell his recruits that once they joined his company, they were "… married to it." He expected complete loyalty and demanded total commitment.

The people he hired projected the image that Philip wanted. He hired under forty, good-looking people, non-smokers, and they had to be fit and trim. They had to fit the Lawco mold, Philip's corporate image.

Philip took an exceptional and personal interest in the hiring of Lawco women. He didn't care so much if they knew how to use a computer. But they had to meet other, more stringent, earthly qualifications; they had to have large breasts and hold a strong propensity to wear short skirts.

He made it a policy to never hire a woman who came to an interview dressed in pants. He thought that women in pants went against human nature.

Philip would sit at his office with binoculars and watch women come and go from the parking lot. If someone was coming in for an interview and was pretty, had large breasts, and were sexually dressed, they would be hired on the spot for whatever position they desired. Once hired, Philip would personally see how many different positions he could *personally* get them into.

Philip was on a conference call in his office when his secretary walked in, "Mr. Lawson," she whispered. "There's someone here to see you."

"I'm on the phone, I don't have time right now."

"She's very insistent."

"I'll have to call you back," Philip announced, and quickly hung up the phone.

"Who is it? He asked his highly paid secretary. He knew she wouldn't disturb him unless she had a very good reason.

"Her name is Cora."

"Cora?" He repeated, trying to think of whom he knew with that name. "I don't think I know any … Cora. What does she want?"

"She said it was personal."

Philip glanced out his open door. There was a dark-haired woman, a very pregnant one at that, pacing back and forth in his outer office. He wracked his brain as to where he knew her from … and then he recalled.

"Let her in."

"Hi, Philip, it's good to see you again," she said sitting down in a leather chair in his office.

"Uh, yeah, it's good to see you, too," it was really more of a question than a statement.

"I'll get right to the point," Cora said, "I just thought you'd like to know ... I'm having your baby."

"You're Stephanie, right?" There'd been so many women in his life he needed a spreadsheet just to keep them straight.

"Is that supposed to be funny? I'm Cora. Cora Lilly. And don't pretend like you don't remember me."

"I don't mean to be crude." Yes, he did mean to be crude, and yes with her that pregnant, he wanted to pretend he had never met her. He just wanted her to go away. "As I was saying, how do I know the baby is mine?"

"There hasn't been anyone else."

"And I'm supposed to believe that?"

"I'm telling the truth," Cora said, reaching into her purse for a tissue.

"You're an unwed mother, how do you plan on raising this child? Did you ever think of getting an abortion?"

"That's a cruel thing to say, to think I came here to tell you this wonderful news, that you're going to be a father."

"That's not something that's exactly in my plans right now."

Tears flowed down Cora's freckled face as Philip got out his checkbook.

Cora took his meager offer and left.

"This is not the end of it," she said. She stuffed the check into her purse without looking at the amount and quickly left his office.

After she left, he tried to work but found himself profoundly disturbed. He strolled around the Lawco office and wandered into the lunchroom, a place he rarely went. A plethora of balloons, streamers, and pink and blue crepe paper adorned the otherwise sterile room.

"What's the occasion?" he asked no one in particular.

"Joshua's wife is pregnant – with twins!"

Philip went into Josh's office.

"Way to go!" Philip said, patting Josh on the back. He tried not to think about the pregnant woman that was just in his office. He wouldn't share *that* news with anyone.

"Thanks Phil. It is pretty exciting. When my wife told me we were having twins, I was bowled over!"

"Yeah … that's great …" Philip said walking out of Joshua's office headed for his own. This was one celebration he wanted no part of, he had an empty feeling in his stomach.

"I don't want to be disturbed," he told his secretary, and then shut the door to his office.

Philip sat down at his desk and read the newspaper. In the local section, there was a small article in the obituary column about socialite Cora Lilly's wealthy uncle passing away, and Cora was the only surviving relative. Shit, he hadn't realized the night he picked Cora up in a bar that she was wealthy in her own right, and now she was even more valuable. As he sat at his desk, it didn't take him long to realize how useful this information was.

Chapter Twelve

Cora screamed. "Screw this natural childbirth, I want drugs - now!"

"Please settle down, Mrs. Lilly." The maternity nurse had seen many difficult women in labor but Cora won the blue ribbon for being a royal pain.

"And my name is not *Mrs.* Lilly, it's *Ms.* Lilly. I'm going to be a single mother, although right now I'm thinking adoption might be an option!"

"Fine *Ms.* Lilly, but I'm afraid you are too far along in your labor to have medication now, you should have asked for it sooner."

"I was going to do this stupid natural method … how was I to know it wouldn't work!"

"Just take some deep breaths, you're almost dilated to ten, pretty soon we'll take you down to the delivery room and you'll be holding your beautiful new baby in your arms."

"Take me now! I want this baby out of me now!"

"Soon. Have some more ice chips and we'll be taking you down soon."

"I don't want anymore damn ice chips, I just want this over with!"

The doctor came into the room and examined Cora. She was ready. Cora was wheeled down on a gurney into the delivery room and her labor continued with her instructions from the doctor to keep pushing until finally her son was born. Matthew.

The next morning, another nurse came into her room with the birth certificate to fill out. Cora looked at it, filled out enough for her satisfaction, and set it aside.

When the nurse came in to collect the paperwork, she glanced it over. "I see you haven't filled out everything, you forgot to fill in the line with the baby's father's name on it." She handed the paper back to Cora, adding in a hushed tone, "the baby needs a father."

The words just hung there like an echo – *the baby needs a father …*

Matthew was asleep next to her in a bassinet. He looked every bit as handsome as his father. He had his father's dark hair and her dimples. She thought about the one night that she had spent with Philip. Sure, it had been one-night stand, but she truly had felt something for him besides his movie star looks and smooth manner.

Matthew was the wonderful gift he had given her. If Philip couldn't or wouldn't give his love, then she would have the next best thing – his child. She only hoped that someday Philip would want her and their child as much as she wanted him.

Cora stared at the blank line, took a deep breath, and filled in the name of Philip Lawson.

The week after she was released from the hospital, Cora swallowed her pride and boldly took her son so his father could meet him.

This time Philip wasn't angry. He held his newborn son in his arms and his standoffish attitude changed in an instant. Not only had an heir been handed to him on a silver platter, Cora's money would come in handy for an up and coming executive such as himself. He made a quick decision to marry this woman he'd only known briefly.

"I'm taking a few days off," he told his secretary.

Philip, Cora, along with baby Matthew took a drive to Reno, where Philip and Cora were married in a quickie ceremony at a wedding chapel. Upon their return, Cora and the baby moved into her newly purchased house, a mansion in the ultra-affluent town of Atherton. Philip liked the locale because it was a good place to live out his self-created image. He knew there was a reason he married Cora, and her checkbook would certainly come in handy.

Chapter Thirteen

Angela Bowman was having a bad day. She was down to her last cigarette in her pack, her cheap bra was not enough support for her silicon implanted breasts, and her underwear was riding up her crotch, giving her an urge to scratch her ass right there in public.

She made a mental note to buy more smokes on the way home from her menial secretarial job at America First, a Japanese Silicon Valley chip company located in the heart of the valley, Santa Clara. She worked as a temp for three months now and she was anxious for more in her life. Her job was going nowhere and besides more cigarettes, she had one other thing on her mind. And she would get what she wanted. She knew that Silicon Valley was the place to find wealth and she was going to get her share one way or another.

She would dispose of her doting husband, Jack Bowman, when the time was right. He was a nuisance. Someone she had to put up with while she planned her future. She knew it had been a mistake marrying him so soon after she graduated high school, but he was older than her, and she mistakenly believed he would be going places. Instead of a career in business as he'd discussed while he was in college and she still in high school, he turned to Civil Service and worked faithfully for the United States Postal Service. She would rid of him when the time was right, but in the meantime, he kept her bed warm and gave her cash. He paid for her breast implants and nose job, but he did not have the kind of money to suit her required lifestyle.

Angela was working through a temporary agency as an administrative assistant. She was only putting in time, waiting for the right opportunity to strike.

When she arrived home that night to her deteriorating East Side apartment, her husband Jack was already home, with dinner ready. Doting Jack was trying to convert her to vegetarianism, tonight's dinner, a tofu and soybean casserole.

It was all Angela could do to avoid throwing up. "Give me a rare hamburger any day," she said.

"Did you say something, dear?"

"I said, what a wonderful treat today."

Angela walked into the kitchen. There were brochures lying across the table. Angela picked them up. She was hopeful. He was going to take her on a cruise or a European vacation. No such luck.

"Sperm Bank Information," read one, "Reversing a Vasectomy," another.

Jack had been married before and had a vasectomy. He didn't want kids when Angela married him, and now he changed his mind and he wouldn't let her forget it.

"I think we should discuss this," Jack said like a puppy wanting a doggie treat.

Angela made a beeline for the bathroom. He was obsessed about having children and she did not want to go into it, at least, not tonight.

Angela yelled from the bathroom, "I had a hard day, I'm going to skip dinner."

She ran a bath, took the Wall Street Journal to read, and warmed up her vibrator. Nothing got her more excited than reading about men who were going places.

She would hunt one down, capture him, and collect the prize money.

She found the article on Philip Lawson, "Silicon Valley Up and Comer," particularly interesting.

Jack went off to his tofu. Angela went off on her hot pink vibrator.

It didn't take Angela long to track down Philip Lawson, it turned out, he was working in the office building next to hers. Her detective work also uncovered where he liked to work out, and that's where she decided to make her move one afternoon.

She artfully positioned herself in the parking lot of the athletic club and waited for just the right moment. And it came when Philip finished his workout and walked out to his car.

"Damn!" she said loudly as he approached.

Philip noticed her immediately. She was wearing skintight black spandex shorts, shorts that showed off her long legs. She wore a lavender colored sleeveless midriff top that clung to her oversize breasts. Her long, shiny black hair accentuated her face. She didn't have a bead of sweat on her, and looked like she belonged in a magazine for men, not standing in a parking lot looking helpless.

"Damn!" she said again. This time much louder to make sure that he heard her.

"Pardon me?" Philip asked her as he put his work out bag down to get a better look at her cleavage that was pouring out of her clinging top that was staring out at him, right into his face, taunting him sexually.

Angela played up to him, "Oh, sorry for my swearing, it's just, well … I'm stuck."

"Stuck?"

"My ride left without me," Angela lied. "Now I'm stuck here. All by myself."

"I'll take you anywhere you want to go," Philip quickly offered.

They went to the Red Corral Restaurant, which was dark inside, even in the middle of the day, a restaurant that had booths in the back where one could sit with a lover in anonymity.

Over red wine and a rare steak, Angela made up an elaborate story about how she was new in town and did not have a job.

He bought it all and hired her on the spot. He could always use another employee with her "assets."

A few days into her new job at Lawco, working as an administrative assistant for the busy Marketing

Department, Angela realized that Philip was falling right into her trap. He was so infatuated with women and enjoyed having his sex that he would not even know what hit him.

It was easy for Angela to take the next step with him. She simply told him her car was in the shop and asked Philip to drive her home. Conveniently, Jack was out of town visiting his relatives. When they arrived at her apartment, she invited him in. *He came into her apartment and into her fifteen minutes later.*

After weeks of having sex with Philip at every given opportunity, Angela thought about her options. She wanted to make sure she had Philip in her back pocket and that she was more than a sex object to him. She knew there was money to be had behind his dark, brooding eyes.

She needed *something* to cement her to him. She needed some way to guarantee her future. She had plans. She had desires. She wanted things, things that a mail carrier could never give her.

When Jack arrived home from work, she was soaking in the tub while she schemed. Jack had abandoned the idea of having more children, but Angela was going to resurrect it.

"Darling." She called out to Jack. Monday Night Football was on and he didn't like to be disturbed.

"Sugar, I've been thinking," Angela said. "And I think we *should* have a baby."

Jack put down his bowl of popcorn, forgot about the game, and jumped up from his recliner. He was surprised, but thrilled. "I'll make all of the necessary arrangements," he said.

The next day Jack made arrangements with the doctor. Angela would see a specialist, and then she would go to the sperm bank and be artificially inseminated.

Jack couldn't wait. He overflowed with joy at the prospect of being a father. He brought gifts for Angela after every scheduled appointment, a stuffed animal, and an infant outfit. Jack couldn't wait to be a father. Angela couldn't wait to be pregnant, either.

She did not tell Jack, however, that she did not want *him* as any form of a father. She also didn't tell Jack that she wasn't keeping her appointments, she didn't need to -- she had her own sperm bank, one that took her on trips and bought her diamonds and gold necklaces, one that didn't require a sterile environment, or legs in cold metal stirrups.

Her sperm bank lived in a huge house in Atherton and had been featured in the Wall Street Journal. Her sperm donor was someone who would pay off big when the time was right.

Chapter Fourteen

The McKenzie family moved out of Fremont, which now included their twins, Sarah and Elizabeth and another baby on the way. The growing family moved into the affluent town of Saratoga where they purchased their first home. It was expensive but Josh assured her they could now afford it.

Marisa loved being pregnant and watching her girls grow and in no time it seemed they went from infants to starting school. In her free time, she volunteered for non-profit organizations. She played tennis once a week, and had her nails and hair done in an upscale salon. She made new friends and always made sure she saw her father when she could.

He would come to their house every week to take care of their yard. He would tease her by saying, "Remember to keep your wits about you and don't overspend." She would shrug him off with a peck on his tan and wrinkled face.

Marisa was thrilled to be living in the same town as her best friend Linda McGregor. Linda still did freelance journalism work yet still made sure she took the time to do the other things she loved, like attending luncheons and playing tennis. Her goal was someday to be a national correspondent but in the meantime, she worked for a local paper and was collecting information in the social circles she was a part of for a novel she was planning on writing.

Marisa called Linda on her cell phone. "You're still coming to the luncheon, right?"

"Of course. I'll be at your house in five minutes."

"What are you wearing?"

"Remember that floral-print dress I bought the other day?"

"How could I forget?"

Marisa thought about how the week before Linda and her went shopping at Stanford Shopping Center in

Palo Alto. Marisa wasn't sure what was more plentiful, the handsome men in their business attire having lunch at outdoor cafes or the pricey clothing boutiques.

Linda pulled up in her two-seater sports car. She had the convertible top down. "Mind if we take your car? My hair is already wind blown enough."

"No problem," Marisa said as they got into her car. Turning to Linda she asked, "Where is the luncheon being held at again?"

Linda laughed. It was an on-going joke between the two friends. "Just follow the Mercedes and Jaguars."

Marisa and Linda stopped at the check in table outside the ballroom of the ritzy hotel to get their nametags. Marisa carefully put hers on, after all she was going to return the designer dress she bought "temporarily" to wear to the charity event.

Marisa glanced into the ballroom, she thought about how the room was filled with corporate widows, and now she was one. Women who filled their days with raising money for charities, lunches, playing tennis and running errands for their working husbands.

She laughed as she thought about how Linda told her when, in her daughter's class at school, the young students were asked what their parents did, one child replied, "My mother runs errands."

Marisa and Linda strolled into the ballroom and could overhear some of the conversations going on around her. "It's hard to fool around when your husband knows everyone." She heard other snippets. "They got their faces done together … we pay our baby sitter in stock options."

"I'll be right back," Linda said. "Can you find us some seats?"

"Sure, no problem."

Marisa saw Sandy, a woman she knew from yoga. "Marisa, you are looking ravishing," Sandy said as she gently kissed Marisa on each of her cheeks.

"Thanks, you know I have good news. I'm pregnant."

"That is fantastic. What's that make it now, four?"

"No, three. I have the twin girls, Sarah and Elizabeth, this will be our third."

"That's right."

The room was filling up fast with women dressed, each set to out do the other in their most fashionable outfits. The waiters were already starting to bring the Caesar salads out. After the entrée, and coffee and dessert, would be a fashion show with students from a local private high school and their mothers serving as models.

"So what's the latest? Got any good gossip?"

"Marisa, you know me better than that! I don't gossip." Then Sandy quickly glanced around to see if anyone was listening. "Have you heard the latest stuff about Gina?"

"Gina?"

"Yeah, she's working her way through all the male realtors in her office. Banging every one of them to snag their prospect list. I mean that woman – if you can call her that, would do anything to get ahead."

"I certainly hope you don't mean that *literally*."

Sandy laughed. "Yes, of course I do. Speak of the devil, there she is now." Sandy motioned her wine glass pointing to a table filled with women, and holding center court – Gina Maxwell."

"Oh God, she's really here? I haven't heard that name in ages."

"Yup, she's here. She's making a name for herself in the real estate market. I'm surprised you haven't heard that. She's becoming one of the most sought after realtors. She's making a bundle, just bought a huge house up on Summit Road, divorced her husband, and now I hear she's on the prowl for a new man to snag, so you better watch out!"

"Believe me, I will."

"Say, where are you sitting?" Sandy asked.

Suddenly Marisa remembered she was supposed to find seats for her and Linda, and most of the tables were already full. "I ..." Marisa glanced around the packed ballroom. "I don't know."

"I'm sitting with Gina but only because I want to pick her brain about buying a new house. You know our house just isn't big enough for us anymore."

Marisa shook her head, both because the shock of seeing Gina again and at the notion Sandy's five thousand square foot house wasn't *big* enough ..."

Linda returned from the restroom and joined Sandy and Marisa. "So what's happening ladies? Are we going to have lunch or what?"

"I'm so sorry Linda, I haven't found a place for us to sit yet," Marisa said with guilt.

Sandy glanced over at the table and mentally counted the chairs. "Why don't you sit at my table, I mean I know Gina is a bitch and all, but if you can stand her for a couple hours, just go put your purses down ..."

"I don't think so." Marisa felt sick to her stomach. "We can find somewhere else to sit."

"Don't be silly," Sandy insisted. "Sit with us."

Hesitantly, Marisa walked over to the table. It had been years since she saw her. Memories came flooding back – when Gina pushed her into the swimming pool. Then there was the time she took her mother's place working at the Greenville's. She didn't know it then, but her mother was dying.

Marisa felt a twinge in her stomach and wondered if it were too soon to feel the baby kick. The last place she wanted to sit was with this haunting face of the past, but she would show her strength and not let Gina get the better of her. Those days were over or so she hoped.

"Hi Gina," Marisa said. "It's been a long time."

Gina was busy chatting with the waiter and ignored her.

Marisa and Linda placed their purses on the table and sat down. The silent treatment from Gina didn't last long.

"You can't sit there! I'm saving those seats for Ducky and Muffy."

Linda leaned over to Marisa. "Sounds like a couple of poodles."

A smile crossed Marisa's face as she realized how inconsequential Gina was to her life. She'd hurt her many times in the past, but she would no longer. Gina liked to play a game that she was better than everyone else, but not this time. This time, Marisa was in control. "We'll sit somewhere else."

Gina turned to face Marisa as they quickly got up to leave. "Ciao."

"Ciao my ass," Marisa whispered to Linda.

Giggling, Linda and Marisa bumped into Victoria, the Chairman of the charity luncheon. "You guys find a place to sit?"

"Yeah, well, we were just going to do that."

"I saved two seats for two of my committee members but they are going to be busy back stage getting ready for the fashion show, so why don't you sit at my table. It's right up front." Victoria nodded over to the table which was clearly had the best location in the room.

"That sounds great," Marisa said.

"Perfect, it'll be fun to have you at my table. It's been ages since we caught up. Better hurry though, 'cause they'll bringing out the entree soon."

"No problem, we're thrilled to sit with you, thanks for asking."

Marisa was not sure what the entree was, but she knew one thing, as she glanced at Gina, that she was the biggest bitch in town.

Chapter Fifteen

As Marisa drove home from the luncheon, what she thought felt like a butterfly twitch in her stomach, had turned into severe cramping. "Linda, I don't think I can drive." Marisa pulled off the freeway and they changed places.

"Are you okay, Marisa?" Linda was worried for her friend. She looked pale, almost gray colored in the face and her eyes were clinched shut like she was in pain.

When Marisa arrived home, she ran to the bathroom where clotted blood darkened the toilet bowl.

Josh knocked on the door. "Dear, what the heck are you doing?"

"Nothing, I'm fine." Only she wasn't fine, and she knew it.

In the morning, Marisa and Josh went to the doctor. The battery of tests was never ending. In the end, they got the news. The nurse led them out of examining room and into the doctor's office. Marisa knew that was not a good sign.

"Well," the doctor began slowly. Marisa counted on Joshua to listen, because she only heard portions of the conversation. A conversation she wanted no part of. The doctor's face said it all. To Marisa the words were burned into her mind that she would never forget. "Spontaneous abortion … give it some time … try again."

As she recuperated, Josh took time off work to care for the twins, and Marisa. He would bring her food and magazines, closed the drapes in the morning, and opened them at night. She wanted it as dark as she felt. She took no phone calls, not even from Linda. She was alone in her depression, in her despair. She blamed herself for the miscarriage, like her father had told her, "Money does not your heart make." She felt her miscarriage was some kind of punishment from God for desiring things she wanted – things she thought would make her life better and now she questioned what was important to her.

She told Josh she was sorry about the baby. He held her in his arms and said he understood. "We are the perfect family just the way we are," he said.

Her recovery was slow, but looking into the garden from her bedroom window, she could see the white daises, which reminded her that even in the darkest of times, life still bloomed.

Chapter Sixteen

The arrival of a designer pair of sunglasses and a tube of luxurious suntan lotion addressed to Marisa, arrived in the mail and she knew what it meant. The following week she received in a plain white envelope, in it a photograph of an unnamed tropical beach. Lawco was sending teasers to the spouses of the employees who were working on making their sales quotas.

Marisa had all but packed her bags. She was sure Josh would make his quota and the annual Lawco trip would be on the horizon. In just a few short weeks, Joshua had in fact made quota as Marisa knew he would, and she was soon debating which outfits to take along for all the occasions she'd need the "right" outfit for.

Marisa debated whether she should throw into her suitcase, a white sexy halter dress that Linda had talked her into buying.

"I've never worn anything like this," she remembered telling Linda.

"All the more reason!" Linda had laughed.

The McKenzie family was soon on their way to Hawaii. The Kihei resort on Maui looked even more beautiful than Marisa imagined. Tall, swaying coconut trees lined the driveway up the main hotel. The ocean was only a few yards away and the beach was private and serene.

While Josh was checking in at the front desk, Marisa saw Adam Tyler. Adam lived in the Marina district in San Francisco, in a Victorian mansion that once belonged to his grandparents. They left the mansion and a fortune to him when they died.

He was young, single, and attractive. He was voted Bachelor of the year by a San Francisco newspaper. Since he inherited his wealth, he only worked for the sport of it. He didn't have to play the game of "getting to the top," like Josh did.

Adam spent his free time playing. He kept a sailboat in Sausalito. He drove a Mercedes-Benz convertible. He vacationed in Aspen with movie stars. He dressed only in the most expensive designer clothes. He could date anyone he wanted, but for some reason, Adam always paid extra attention to Marisa. When he spoke to her, she felt like a woman again.

She loved the way Adam paid attention to her, and if she didn't know better, she would think that he liked her.

Josh never noticed of course, he was always too busy making the next business contact. Adam was one of the most attractive men she had ever met, and he had a sensuality about him that aroused an interest in Marisa.

When he looked at Marisa, his eyes seem to look deep into her soul. Marisa remembered a time when her husband looked at her like that. Those days seem long ago now. Between Josh's work and the girls, there just never seemed to be enough time, enough looks.

After pleasantries were exchanged between the trio, Josh excused himself. "I see someone I want to say hello to." Then he took off toward a group he wanted to ingratiate himself into.

The girls were busy running around the lobby getting their pent up energies released.

Marisa had one problem with Adam. She couldn't look at him. He was simply too handsome.

"I love your haircut," Adam said, as he took his fingers and playfully stroked her hair.

"You do? Josh hates it. He was so mad when I came home with it cut a few weeks ago. You know Joshua. He doesn't like change. He wanted me to keep my hair long and straight, like when I was eighteen."

"Well, he's in the dark ages. You look really beautiful to me."

Who me? Thought Marisa. It had been a long time since Marisa felt pretty, if ever. Adam had a way of making her feel like a beautiful woman. He stirred feelings in her that made her ache to feel loved. Her relationship with her husband had become almost platonic, robotic, day in and day out the same thing. With Adam, she longed to be free and to let herself go in a way that she would feel too self-conscious with her own husband.

"So, is Josh still all work and no play?" Adam said, his brown eyes staring at Marisa as if he were undressing her.

"Yup, you know Josh, he never stops, and he's either out of town or at some important meeting." Marisa blushed. Her body felt a wave of electricity run through it. She fanned her face as she tried to cool herself down.

"Listen," Adam said, "Did you bring your own tennis racquet?"

"Of course, I wouldn't think of coming to Hawaii without it."

"Okay. Then it's a date. While you are here, let's play around some. Tennis, that is."

Marisa laughed. "That would be fun."

Marisa congratulated Adam on his being chosen as Bachelor of the Year by a San Francisco magazine, and then noticed the twins were making a bee-line for the exit doors. "I've got to run."

"See you later Mari."

"Okay. See you later."

Adam kissed Marisa on her cheek and her entire body felt warmed by that simple kiss Adam had given her. He excited her very being.

Josh approached her. "What was that all about?"

"Nothing," Marisa said as she took her daughter's hand. "You know Adam, always the flirt." She giggled as she thought about how Adam made her feel so sexy, a feeling she hadn't felt in a long time.

"Come on girls," Marisa said to the twins. "Let's take the elevator up to the room and change before we check you into the day camp. Dad and I are going to go for a drive."

"Can we go for a swim?" Sarah asked.

"Of course you can, it's part of the day camp program. You'll have lots of fun. There are tons of activities for you to do. You'll probably even see some dolphins."

"Let's go," Elizabeth said, grabbing her sisters' hand as the two girls raced to the elevator.

Josh rented a car and he and Marisa spent the rest of the afternoon driving around the island. They explored hidden beaches and coffee bars. They stopped in a small village, strolled down the wooden sidewalk, and Marisa window-shopped. Marisa stopped and stared in a shop window and stared at a figurine of a woman holding two children in her arms.

Joshua noticed Marisa wiping tears from her eyes. He put his arm around her. "Are you okay?"

"I'm fine … really."

"What's wrong? I can tell when something's bothering you. You've been acting funny all day."

Marisa wiped tears away. "Nothing. I'm fine."

"That is a beautiful statuette. It reminds me of you and the girls. Why don't I go in and see how much it costs," Josh said.

"No, no, it's fine. Let's just get back to the hotel."

Later that night, after the rest of the Lawco employees and their spouses or "guests" had arrived, there was a luau, followed by dancing and much drinking. The invitation called for "Hawaiian casual dress." Josh wore a brightly colored, loose fitting Hawaiian shirt and shorts. Marisa thought he looked handsome, but the other men weren't in Hawaiian wear, opting instead for casual knit polo short-sleeved shirts and long pants.

Josh and Marisa walked into the ballroom where the dinner was being held. "Love your shirt, Josh," a drunken Philip yelled out, laughing.

The band playing was an aging San Francisco rock band, whose members could qualify for the Denny's senior discount breakfast, but they had to make a living somehow. Philip had them flown out just for his occasion.

The leader of the band was yelling, getting everyone even more *pumped* up than they already were. "You're successful ... Beautiful people," and then the obligatory "Are you having a good time?" to which everyone cheered. Then they put in a plug, "When Lawco's rolling out your new product, we'll be rolling out our new album."

Philip smiled when the band managed to work "Lawco" into the lyrics of one of their songs. Marisa felt like she was in the middle of a beer commercial.

All the flowing alcohol, made Marisa have to go to the bathroom. Inside the ladies room, two women were talking. They were both dressed in expensive black sequined dresses and primping their dyed blonde hair.

Marisa sat in the stall and listened.

"Philip really looks good tonight doesn't he?" said one giggling.

"I think the affair he's having with Angela agrees with him."

"Do you think Cora knows?"

One of the bathroom stall doors came flying open. "What are you talking about?"

"Mrs. Lawson, I didn't see you come in."

"Obviously not!"

Cora stormed out of the bathroom with a trail of toilet paper stuck to the heel of her shoe.

"This ought to be good," Marisa said to herself as she washed her hands quickly.

The women followed an enraged Cora out to the ballroom. Cora was filled with fury as she searched for her husband.

Angela was wearing a white low-cut sleeveless dress that clung to her body and showed off her dark tan and overflowing breasts. Her long black hair was tousled about, flowing with every dance move. Her body was moving in harmony with Philip's, just like when they had sex.

Cora pushed Angela away. "You bitch!"

The beer chugging and dancing came to a standstill. All eyes were on the company President, his wife, and his mistress.

"Cora, I was just dancing with Angie," Philip said with an innocent look in his dark brown eyes.

"I'm not stupid. The whole company knows about you and Angela!"

Philip pouted. "I don't know what you're talking about. I was just dancing, what's the big deal?"

Cora burst into tears. Philip helped a normally strong, but now weeping Cora off the dance floor. He would have to convince her of his innocence. He would wait until she calmed down, and he would admit to nothing.

After Philip took Cora back to their suite, she would forgive him, and Philip would see to it, she had too. He needed her inheritance.

Angela made an unobtrusive exit from the dance floor. She found herself in the hotel bar. She ordered a double olive martini. On her second drink, she noticed Wayne Darcy, from Yakima. He was by himself. His timid wife wasn't with him.

Angela took her drink over and slid into the booth with Wayne. Her night would not be a total loss.

Marisa found the commotion between Philip, his wife, and his girlfriend quite entertaining. Bets were being taken if Cora would forgive him or not.

Marisa didn't know how Philip found time to run a successful company and women at the same time. She didn't know how he could be such a snake and how Josh couldn't see that side of him. She decided she didn't want to think about it, and told Josh she wanted to go back to the hotel room.

"I'm not ready to go yet." He still had people to meet and networks to link.

Disgusted, Marisa headed up to the room alone. She wandered down the tiki light path that led to the hotel rooms.

The breeze was warm and made her feel good.

She soon ran into Adam.

"Hey, where are you off to?"

"I'm going to bed," she said.

"Alone?" he asked with interest.

"I was on my way to the Lanai Club," Adam said. "Why don't you go with me?"

"Really?" She thought about his offer for a moment. "No, I'm tired, I'm going to call it a night."

As an afterthought, she asked him, "Did you see that scene in there with Philip?"

Adam laughed and shook his head. He said softly, "Marisa, can I give you some advice?"

"Of course."

"You should celebrate a little. Be a party girl. Let loose, for once."

Marisa thought he was getting too personal, quickly she said, "I have to go."

"If you change your mind, I'll be in the Lanai Club, I'll buy you a drink."

"Okay, good night," Marisa said as she headed for her room.

"Good night, my dear," Adam's voice trailed off.

The hotel room was quiet when she entered it. The girls were sound asleep. Megan, the hotel baby sitter was reading a book. She paid the sitter and the sitter left.

Marisa lay down on the bed. She was tired, but her mind was racing.

Why does Philip always get away with everything? Why would a handsome guy like Adam Tyler flirt with me? Why do I always do the right thing? Why am I a good girl and not a party girl? Marisa wanted to feel sensuous again. She had been through so much pain in her life; she wanted to feel alive again.

Marisa lay on the bed and thought about Adam. She thought about Josh. He was the love of her life. However, she was thinking about Adam.

She lay in bed and waited for Josh to come back. She looked at the clock. It was late. She briefly thought about going back out to have a drink with Adam, just one drink.

But Marisa had her role to play. She was a good girl, a good wife and a good mother. She was definitely not, *a party girl.*

She leaped up from the bed, "Screw it!" she said as she threw off the conservative concealing outfit she had been wearing and put on the sexy low cut halter dress she brought. She got dressed in record time.

With sandals in hand, she ran out of the room and into the hotel hallway. "Megan, wait, I need you a little longer."

The Lanai Club was dark. It took her a moment for her eyes to adjust. The Club was wall-to-wall people. The music was pounding. Marisa took a deep breath.

What have I got myself in for? She wondered. Across the dance floor, she saw him. Handsome with his dark tanned firm body. He had hair that she longed to run her fingers through. White dress shirt, with the sleeves rolled up. No Hawaiian shirt for him. Slip on Italian leather loafer shoes. No socks. "What am I doing here?" she silently asked herself, again. She turned around to leave, when someone stopped her. It was Adam.

"I knew you'd change your mind."

"I couldn't sleep."

"Let's go over here," he said, taking her hand.

"A bottle of champagne please," he told the passing waiter.

They chatted forever. They talked about everything except the computer software business. Many drinks later, he took her hand, and said, "let's go for a walk."

They walked down a narrow pathway lined with palm trees. The moon was their only light. At the end of the path was a romantic beach area. They sat down and said nothing.

With only the crashing waves as background music, they fell against the warm sand. They looked at the stars in silence. Then it happened. Marisa felt Adam's hand on her thigh. She knew she should protest, but she did not. He worked his way up her dress with his hands. When he got to where there should have been panties, there were none. He was pleasantly surprised.

Marisa undid his belt buckle and the top button of his pants. Adam finished what she started.

He unzipped his pants and she pulled them down. He lifted her dress and caressed her breasts.

She melted into the sand as he gave her a passionate kiss. There was no turning back. She was his. He was hers. He entered her, like he belonged there.

Then Marisa heard a voice, a man's voice -- Joshua's voice.

Chapter Seventeen

"Marisa, move over." Josh was annoyed. His wife had fallen asleep on his side of the hotel bed.

"And don't you want to take your clothes off?"

"I'm fine …" The thoughts of the evening ran through her mind. Only it was just a dream. It wasn't real. It was just a fantasy. Having fallen asleep in her clothes on the bed, she was soon brought back to reality by Josh waking her out of her slumber. She thought of Adam as she got out of bed and removed her dress and slipped back into the bed. Perhaps if she fell back to sleep quickly she could resume her fantasies of her and Adam on the beach …

Upon their return from Hawaii, everyone resumed their daily routine. Marisa - a Silicon Valley wife. Josh – a businessman who dreamed of the brass ring. Philip, who believed he could conquer the world and keep both mistresses and a wife happy at the same time. And Adam - with his nonchalant way of being.

Philip did get off easy with Cora, as he knew he would. One shopping trip to New York and she was a new woman. He could connive his way out of any predicament. He laughed at how easy it was to keep Cora happy. She just wanted money and things. She just wanted her position as Mrs. Philip Lawson.

While Cora was in New York shopping, Philip took Angela out to lunch. To the Red Corral Restaurant. They had one of the private booths in the back of the restaurant.

Philip began the conversation with an apology for his wife's behavior in Hawaii. While they were waiting for their food, Philip gave Angela a gift. A diamond studded tennis bracelet. She accepted his apology.

Angela thanked him by running her tongue across his lips. Then, purposely dropped her napkin to the floor. She leaned to pick it up and went under the table. The tablecloth hid her body. She unzipped Philip's pants and gave him dessert. In the parking lot after, they sat in his car and shared a marijuana cigarette.

They were back to work by two. By two-thirty Philip sent out a corporate wide memo - Angela Bowman was now a Vice President of Lawco.

Angela was thrilled, but she wanted more than a diamond tennis bracelet and the title of Vice President. She wanted more than relieving Philip Lawson's erection under a table at the Red Corral Restaurant.

Chapter Eighteen

Marisa was troubled. She could not stop thinking about the dream she had in Hawaii. The dream she had about her and Adam on the beach. Making love. The dream she had after she had fallen asleep on the bed waiting for Josh. Waiting for him to come back from the party, to come back from his networking.

Marisa unpacked her suitcase from the Hawaii trip. She found at the bottom of her suitcase something wrapped in tissue paper. The white porcelain statuette that she had seen in the window, the figurine of a woman and two children, the one that made her cry, the one she had fallen in love with. She read the note. "Darling, I am so sorry about the baby. Always remember that I love you. Please know that we are a perfect family just the way we are. Love, J."

After wiping her tears away, she folded the note and tucked the note into a hole on the bottom of the statuette. Then she placed her newest treasured memento on the top of her dresser where it would always remind her of Joshua's unrelenting love for her.

Chapter Nineteen

"Guess what darling?" Angela came into the apartment beaming. "I've just come back from the doctor's office, and they confirmed it, I'm pregnant!"

Jack was thrilled. The insemination worked. Just as he knew it would. Angela would have his baby and they would be a family after all.

However, for Angela, her plan was just beginning. She would collect on it when the time was right, but not quite yet.

Angela told everyone at Lawco the good news.

"I hear you're expecting," Philip said when she walked into his office. Just out of curiosity, who's the father?"

Angela laughed in a mocking tone. "Jack is of course!"

He doubted her for a moment, and then shrugged the thought off -- he had too much work to do, he was busy with meetings, deadlines, and release dates of software.

As months passed, and Angela got bigger and bigger, Philip became less interested in her. He did not want to have sex with a pregnant woman, not even phone sex.

When the baby was born, Angela and Jack named her, Alexandra. Angela took a six-week maternity leave and then returned to work. The first thing Angela did at the office was to put a picture of Alexandra on her desk. Alexandra had jet-black hair, just like her father. She had his smile, his hair, and every one of his beautiful facial features.

Employees of Lawco would walk by her desk and glance at the picture, with knowing smirks.

Marisa came to the office to drop off Joshua's briefcase that he had forgotten at home. He had been working long hours and had been getting forgetful. It wasn't unusual for him to work seventy to eighty hour weeks, as was the case for anyone wanting to get ahead in Silicon Valley, it was the norm, the expected.

Marisa walked by Angela's desk where Angela was staring aimlessly at her computer monitor.

"Angela, how are you?" Marisa said.

"I'm great. I'm glad to be back from maternity leave. Oh," Angela said reaching for a framed photo on her desk. "Here's a picture of my little darling. He is handsome, but then I am biased." A sly smile crossed Angela's lips.

The thought went through Marisa's head that the rumors of Philip being the father were in fact true. The baby had a resemblance to him that was uncanny. "He is a cutie," Marisa said. Then she walked into Joshua's office. "Here's your briefcase," she said as she gave him a tentative kiss.

"You're late," Joshua said, "You're always late." He was not in a good mood.

Marisa tried to change the subject, "Have you seen the picture of Angela's baby?"

"Of course I have," Joshua said annoyed that he had forgotten his briefcase and now his wife probably wanted to go to lunch, which he didn't have time for.

"You didn't notice anything unusual about it?"

"No, I didn't." Actually, Joshua had never even looked at the picture.

"Don't you see the resemblance?"

"What are you talking about?" Joshua was checking his briefcase to make sure all his papers were still in it. He said he was late for a meeting and had to go.

Marisa left the office, wondering why Josh would not see Philip for what he really was, a womanizing prince of darkness. She believed there was a genuine evil lurking behind those dark eyes of his.

Joshua left the office wondering why Marisa was always against Philip. He thought she was unreasonable in her dislike for him.

Josh took the notes Marisa had recently pulled out from her college days, hoping Josh would start his own company. He worked them into a formal proposal for Philip without telling his wife that he had planned to show it to his boss. He had been working on it night and day. He wanted it refined before he presented it.

Since Philip was his original mentor, he did not want to go solo even though that was what Marisa wanted. He wanted Philip to be a part of the venture; he knew he was someone who could help him get the business off the ground. The business would be a success and Marisa would be pleased that her idea would be brought to fruition, even if it meant working with Philip.

Joshua started the meeting with Philip by telling him he thought Lawco was in trouble. "Philip, I didn't say anything when my expense checks were late, and I wasn't getting reimbursed, but, when my paycheck was late, I started to analyze the problem, just like I would study business economics in college."

Joshua suggested they start by cutting back, temporarily until they regrouped, then re-hire when they needed to. Joshua told him that they could implement his idea for new software, the one that would make businesses run more efficiently. He told Philip he was concerned Lawco was making the number one mistake start-up companies face. Growing too fast too soon. "It can take up to six start-up attempts, before one is actually successful," Joshua told Philip. "So don't feel so bad."

"Me feel bad? You don't know me at all do you?" How dare this pipsqueak come into his office and tell him how to run his business.

Sure, Philip knew the initial money he put into Lawco was going fast, and Cora now had all but closed her checkbook to him. And yes they needed capital to stay in business, cash to stay afloat, long enough to go public, which had always been his goal.

"We need a new idea, a new vision ... a new plan in the form of a new, fresh company."

"Do we now?" Philip would let Joshua run off at the mouth, hear him out before telling him to get the hell out of his office. Joshua went on like he was giving a classroom lecture. Philip was stunned when he heard a litany of what Josh thought were all his faults; Philip's extravagant lifestyle, his houses, wife, mistresses, condo in the city, and Philip's latest acquisition, a private jet.

Then Joshua showed him the proposal. "I'll think about it," he said. "Just leave it with me for now and I'll look it over."

"Don't forget," Joshua reminded him. "Party at my house on Friday night."

"Right." Did Joshua think he needed reminding now of his appointments. What was with this guy? Suddenly he turned into someone telling *him* what to do? He'd go to the idiot's Joshua's house all right, he needed to keep Josh at bay until he had the deal for the new company signed, sealed and delivered – to himself.

"How was your day?" Josh asked when he arrived home, proud of himself that he at last had confronted Philip about the sinking ship of Lawco and presented him with *his* plan to start a new company. But the sour look on Philip's face had told him perhaps he'd gone too far in detailing Philip's shortcomings.

"It was fine. Nothing new." He quickly changed the subject. "How are the plans for the party coming?"

"The party?"

"You didn't forget did you? You know throwing parties are all part of getting ahead."

"Oh, the party, no of course I didn't forget." She had forgotten but she didn't tell him that. "I've got it under control."

The next morning, Marisa met Linda for coffee.

"Linda, I need your help," Marisa confided as she drank her café latte. "I have to give a dinner party for some business people and it has to be perfect."

"And," Marisa added, "of course, I expect you to be there."

"I wouldn't miss this. I'm dying to meet this Mr. Philip Lawson, you keep talking about."

"The snake himself?"

"That's right."

Marisa liked Linda because she had not let her wealth go to her head; she had befriended Marisa and took her under her wing, and was helping her learn how to walk through the maze.

"Use Rose Florist, for the flowers, and Swan's for the catering. Swan's is known for their handsome men dressed in tuxedos who love to serve the women of the valley."

Marisa laughed, "Linda, is that all you can ever think about?"

"Oh, yeah," she said changing the subject. "I know a great jazz band you can hire, too."

Marisa was grateful for her help. Marisa wrote down all of her ideas on a small notebook she carried in her purse.

"Go to Raphael's Art Studio, in town, they will lend you some art pieces on approval, after the party, you just return them."

After Linda told Marisa all the places to go for her party, they talked about the latest gossip, Linda then told Marisa about a divorce party she was invited to. The divorcing couple lived in wealthy Los Altos Hills. It was the last weekend the husband had in the house before the divorce deadline his wife had given him. He decided to have a big blowout and invite everyone he knew.

Linda told Marisa how the couple had only recently bought the huge house in Los Altos Hills. She said the husband wanted to show it off at least once before he had to leave it.

Linda laughed as she asked Marisa what kind of gift she should take for a "divorce party."

"They have everything material," Linda said, "They made a killing when the IPO was released. He exercised some of his options as soon as he could, while the price was at its highest."

Marisa drank her latte, amazed. She had so much to learn.

"Anyway," Linda continued, "now, the stock has floundered."

"Why are they getting a divorce?"

"I don't know, maybe she found someone else whose stock is worth more." They laughed and finished the last of the chocolate croissants and their lattes.

Marisa thanked Linda, and took her notebook full of ideas; she had a busy day ahead.

The night of the party, the guests started arriving at six. Marisa and the caterers had the food and entertainment planned precisely. Marisa wanted to make sure everything was perfect for her husband's sake.

The guests started with hors d'oeuvres in the backyard by the swimming pool. The jazz band was playing lightly in the background. There was just enough music to not interfere with the mostly business conversations.

Cora, who was standing close to Philip, was telling Marisa and Linda about her latest charity event, something about saving the dolphins.

Philip turned to Marisa and asked her about a painting on a wall in the house. "Can you tell me about the artist?"

Marisa blushed when she realized she didn't know anything about the artist, nothing at all, the only thing she knew was that she had borrowed the painting from the art studio.

"I have to check on something." Marisa turned away, her cheeks flushed.

"I'll tell you about the painting." Linda was more than happy to oblige.

Marisa mouthed a "thank you," to her friend and then hurried away. She walked into the house and glanced out the living room window. She was mortified to see her father with his truck parked out front, filled with his gardening equipment. He had his head down as he was blowing leafs from the driveway.

"Dad, I guess I forgot to tell you, we're having a party, can you come back tomorrow?"

"What?"

"We're having a party. This is not a good time to be doing the yard."

"Today was such a nice day, and I wasn't busy with anything else so I thought I'd come a day early. Oh, by the way, I just met one of your guests."

"You did?" Marisa wondered how long until the gossip spread that her gardener was in fact her father.

"Perhaps I can join you all when I'm finished here."

"I don't think that's such a good idea. I mean you're not really dressed for the occasion." He was wearing denim overalls and an orange T-shirt underneath. His tennis shoes had holes in the toes and he was wearing a Giants baseball cap, on backyards.

"How about for just a little while? I could use something to eat."

Marisa lost her composure. The words slipped out before she recognized what she had said. "Go home, Dad, now!"

"Excuse me?"

"I'm sorry Dad, I didn't mean that …"

"Don't worry about it," he said, gathering up his tools. Charlie got the message ... he definitely got the message. And his heart was breaking.

Chapter Twenty

As Charlie drove away from his son-in-law and daughter's prestigious home, the realization sunk in that he was no longer a significant part of her life. She had dismissed him as if he was the hired help, and his heart ached. The Silicon Valley lifestyle Marisa so longed for as a child now seemed to have consumed her very being as an adult.

He couldn't help but wonder what Cassie would think of her daughter now? Would she think he had failed as a father? He raised Marisa the best way a single father could. The thought of re-marriage never entered

his mind. No one could or would ever replace Cassandra
… his beautiful Cassandra.

Replaying the first night he met his Cassie over
offered him comfort and he felt closer to her when he
thought of her and the love they shared, the children
they made, the bond that couldn't be broken no matter
how hard people had tried. He remembered that first
night that he met her as if it were yesterday …

Overseeing the last minute preparations of the
Hillsborough grounds, for which he was in charge,
anticipation was in the air for the party that was to follow
Cassandra Thoroughgood's entry into society.

Charlie, working as the caretaker, wanted to make
sure everything was perfect. Even though he wouldn't be
a guest, he had a soft spot in his heart for the spirited,
auburn beauty, Cassie.

Cassie had been in her luxurious bedroom on the
second floor of the Thoroughgood estate, being hand-
stitched into her ball gown.

"Cassandra Jean, you must be still." Mitzi said.

Cassie had other things on her mind than her
presentation into society. The only society she wanted to
be a part of was one that was not so stuffy and rigid. She

wanted to be eligible to marry of course, and of course, she *wanted* a man. Still a virgin, she ached to be held by a man with muscular arms, kissed by a man with loving, tender lips, taken for the first time – by a man she loved.

A life that Cassie wanted no part of was being planned for her, right down to the final stitches in her hand-sewn dress. She would enter society as a debutante, engagement to follow by a lavish wedding. She, her husband, and any children they had would be photographed for every society magazine and of course for her father's newspaper empire.

"Just one moment, please Mitzi," Cassie pleaded as she felt as though she couldn't breath as the tightening of the dress only confirmed the imprisoned life that she was expected to lead.

"Whatever ya say, Ma'am." Mitzi knew when to back off with Cassie. One push too many and she would be impossible to deal with. She already was a handful. Had been ever since the day the Mr. and Mrs. Thoroughgood brought her home from the hospital. Mitzi had been busy ever since trying to raise her in the best way she, a nanny, could.

"I'll give you a minute. But then we must finish the dress," Mitzi said as she handed Cassie a handkerchief dampened with water.

Mitzi left the room and Cassie took the cloth and held it against her skin. She walked over to the open window and breathed in the fresh air. The peninsula fog was just beginning to roll in, it made her feel rejuvenated, as if she just wanted to run outside, run away from the confinement of what the party held, what her life held. Run away and never look back.

Charlie was finishing his last minute walk through of the massive grounds when he glanced up to the second floor and noticed Cassandra had pushed her lace curtains aside and was leaning out of her window.

Cassie dropped the handkerchief, which landed near his feet.

"Sorry, Mr. Taft."

"No problem, Miss Cassandra. I'll just put it right here," Charlie said as he placed it on a wicker chair.

"Wait, Mr. Taft, I'll be right down. Mitzi will kill me if I lose one of her fine linens."

"You know to call me Charlie," he said with a chuckle. He looked up but she had disappeared.

As Cassie came down the staircase, she caught a glimpse of her father in his study. He was smoking a cigar and talking on the telephone, "The photographer needs to be here in twenty minutes or he's fired!"

Cassie saw her mother walk authoritatively into the kitchen. "Everything needs to be perfect. Don't you people understand?"

The servants had been working all day to make sure the food and silverware was all in place. They spent hours polishing and buffing every piece of silver and crystal throughout the mansion. They were hoping if all went well, they would all receive significant bonuses. The servants knew that James Thoroughgood was a self-made man and knew the value of rewarding those that worked hard for him.

Cassie had been secretly in love with their gardener for years. She admired his muscles, his dark hair and sparkling brown eyes. She loved the way he would recite poetry while he was working on the yard.

"Mr. Taft, wait!" Cassie ran to him in her bare feet and white ball gown.

Charlie smiled. He was captivated by her presence and by her beauty. Her freckles that he once knew had disappeared, and left a radiant, glowing skin. Her flowing auburn hair glistened and smelled like honeysuckle. The ball gown she had on accentuated her petite figure. He was not sure how it happened, but sometime during the last three years, she had grown into a beautiful woman.

Cassie boldly took Charlie by his hand and led him down a lane and into an empty pool house where they passionately made love.

Cassandra was presented into society later that evening as planned but she had no plans to marry one of the men her father had picked out for her. She had already lost her virginity to a man she had adored for years, a man that would never meet with the approval of her parents, but it was a man she had fallen passionately in love with.

She met Charlie every week for months in the pool house. Every week, their love for each other grew stronger and stronger.

Her father was furious when he learned of their affair, threatening to cut off her trust fund.

"I don't care what you do. I love Charles, and I'm going to marry him!"

"If you ever married him, I would not only disinherit you – I would disown you as my daughter. I would never acknowledge your presence ever again!"

"Father, you don't frighten me, I will choose love over money, any day."

The next time Charlie went to the estate, James called Charlie into his den. The room was filled with animal heads and photographs of James with a variety of world famous people. He was just finishing a phone call, "Thank you for everything, Dr. Bernstein."

"Here," James said, as he handed Charlie a check. "Get out and don't come back."

Charlie stared at it in disbelief, a check made out to Charles Taft for fifty thousand dollars. "You have to be kidding." Charlie ripped it up and threw it at James.

"I am dead serious, take this money and get out of here now!"

"Just because you *have* money, you think you can control who your daughter loves? And to think, I came here to ask you for Cassandra's hand in marriage."

"I think you're the one that's kidding. My daughter would never marry you!"

"Your daughter loves me and we will marry!"

James started to write out another check. "How much do you want? I will give you whatever you want. Cassandra is a Thoroughgood and would never marry someone of your station in life."

"It'll be all right Cassie." Mitzi said as she gave a weeping Cassie a hug. Mitzi then hurriedly packed

Cassie's suitcase with just the necessary clothes. She'd be needing new ones anyway soon, ones that would fit her and her soon to be growing belly.

Downstairs, the voices emanating from the den were getting louder and louder. "How dare you take advantage of my daughter the way you have?"

"I love Cassie and I will marry her."

"You will not!" James opened a drawer where he kept a pistol and aimed it directly at Charlie's chest. "You will never see my daughter again!"

Charlie bolted from the room and headed up the staircase. "Cassie, I'm coming for you!"

Mitzi grabbed Cassie and stopped her from running out the bedroom. "But, I love him."

"It's the way it has to be," Mitzi said.

James quickly ran after Charlie as he ran up the stairs. A struggle ensued. The pistol went off, leaving Charlie shot in the leg. He was bleeding profusely.

"Now, get out of here once and for all," James said, still holding the pistol toward Charlie.

Charlie limped out the front door and shouted up to the second floor. "Cassie, I love you, and I will be back for you!"

Charlie flagged down a passing car who took him to the nearest hospital where they were able to stop the bleeding from his leg -- but not from his heart. The police refused to file any charges against James Thoroughgood, as he was not one to fool with.

A month later, Charlie snuck back onto the property. He saw Mitzi outside. "I need to see her."

"She's not here."

"Please. Tell me where she is."

"Mr. Thoroughgood sent her away. All I can say is she is living back East."

Charlie packed his pickup truck and drove across the country. He went to every private school he could find. Some were tucked away in private, mountainous, areas so high that his truck had trouble making it up their winding roads.

Several were behind locked gates and he would park his truck outside and then jump over the fence to get close to the school. Twice security guards threatened him. When he told them his story, they felt sorry for him, but unfortunately told him that there was no Cassandra Thoroughgood there. Charlie never knew if they were lying or telling the truth. He chose to believe them, what else could he do?

Charlie spent months traveling the Eastern states searching for Cassie. His heart openly ached for her.

When his money ran out, he turned his truck west and headed back to California. On the way out of Massachusetts, he got a flat tire. He was soon covered in grime and the jack kept slipping.

"Please God," he cried out. "Help me find Cassandra ..."

He lay saddened with an acceptance that Cassie was never to be in his life again when a car pulled up behind his truck and stopped.

"Can I assist you?"

Charlie glanced up and saw a nun, covered head to toe in a black habit.

Charlie left his truck on the side of the road, and drove with her in her car back to her convent. Once there, she gave him food and a much-needed shower.

"Sister Beatrice, how can I ever thank you?"

"There is something, if you aren't in a hurry to get anywhere? We really could use a little handyman work around here."

"Sounds like a plan to me." He was in no hurry to return to California now. What is this place anyway?"

"We run a home for unwed mothers."

"Oh, I see ..."

When they went to the cafeteria to have lunch, Charlie glanced around the room, and by the grace of

God, he had found his beloved Cassie. He was stunned but felt blessed to discover she was pregnant. Her father had sent her away when he found out that she was expecting a child, and had arranged through Dr. Bernstein to have the bastard child given up for adoption.

Charlie asked Cassie to marry him, and she said yes. After their wedding vows were exchanged, they lived at the Convent until Johnathan was born. After his birth, they drove back to California and settled in a small house in San Jose, where Charlie had lived ever since. They had never heard from her parents ever again, until that night Charlie called her father to tell him she had died.

As Charlie pulled his truck into his driveway of the house he had lived in all these years, he said a prayer for Joshua and Marisa. He hoped Joshua would be able to give Marisa the life she dreamed of, and he prayed that she would not get hurt in the process.

After taking a cold beer out of the refrigerator, he went to his closet and picked up the metal box from the floor, underneath a stack of shoes.

Taking the box and beer in hand, he sat in his comfortable recliner in front of the TV. One by one, he pulled out items from the box. This was not the first time he did. He would pull the box out and look through it when he was filled with despair. He didn't know why he did, but it had become a habit to him. Then he would have a good, silent, private cry. He set aside the envelope that was filled with his son's belongings, all that was left from the night he died. He never opened the envelope, nor would he ever. Instead, he read a note his wife had written him before she died, "I love you as deep as the ocean is blue, and my heart is yours. Thank you for rescuing me and teaching me what love is. Love, Cassie." He reached for the phone to call his daughter. He did not like the way they had left it. He wanted to remind her how important family is, and how quickly life goes by. She had been so rude to him, and he was sure she would have called by now and apologized but since she hadn't, he'd call her. "Oh God," Charlie cried out, as a heavy pressure came over his chest. The note fell out of his hand, and he dialed 911, before he collapsed.

Chapter Twenty-One

Marisa floated restfully upon her air mattress letting her manicured hands dip gracefully in the pools comforting water. Later, she would call Linda and they would re-hash every detail of the prior evening. She made a mental note when she got out of the pool to call her father, she regretted about how badly she had spoken to him.

"Hello? Anybody home" A male voice called out from the backyard gate.

"So much for trying to get in a few rays," Marisa said with a wide smile as she pulled herself gracefully from the pool.

"Hi Adam," a dripping Marisa said. "What's up?"

"It's nice to see you, too."

She laughed. "It is good to see you too!"

Marisa put a towel around her waist as they stood there, like a couple meeting for the first date.

"Love your suit."

Marisa blushed, almost embarrassed. She was wearing her tiniest bikini.

She looked away while adjusting the towel around her waist, just to cleanse her thoughts of how just looking at him had made her go moist between her legs.

"I'm sorry if I disturbed you, Marisa. But I had to drop off this report for Josh," he awkwardly explained.

She took it from him and placed it carelessly on the patio table. "He's playing golf today."

"Well, enjoy your sun-bathing," Adam said, heading out the back gate.

"I will …"

Adam was reaching for the door of his Mercedes, when she stopped him. "You sure I can't get you anything?"

"Sure, that would be great." Adam followed her back into the yard. "So you got rid of Josh, what about the twins?"

"They won't be home for hours," Marisa smiled. She picked up her suntan lotion. "Do me a favor?"

"Anything."

She grinned a little more and handed him the sun-warmed tube of SPF 40.

Adam accepted the creamy sunscreen. It was an invitation, an open invitation. One that Adam deeply wanted.

Marisa's body melted when Adam's sparkling brown eyes looked into hers. Her body quivered and she knew – her most secret fantasies were about to come alive. With the first touch of his gentle hand to her back, she leaned in and kissed him full on his lips. He responded passionately to her kiss that left Marisa's body tingling like there would never be a new tomorrow.

Adam slipped the bikini top from her breasts revealing taut nipples. He licked slowly around them with a demanding tongue. His hands reached down and he removed the bottom of her bikini that she wriggled away from her feet, tossing it off to the side. She wrapped her legs around his. She held him close. She didn't close her eyes. She wanted to see every inch of him. Every muscle. They made love like she'd never experienced before.

They climaxed together. As moisture dripped down Marisa's leg, she heard the back yard gate open.

"Mom, we're home!"

The girls startled Marisa as she fell off the air mattress and out of her dream.

"Mom, get out of the pool. The phone is ringing, and we're hungry!"

"I'll be right there!" Marisa grabbed a towel on her way into the house to take the call.

"Is this Marisa Taft?"

Marisa was still reeling from her dream of Adam and was perturbed her fantasy had been interrupted. "Taft was my maiden name," she said. "My name is McKenzie now."

"Well, Mrs. McKenzie." There was a long pause. "I'm Dr. Dirksen."

"Yes?"

"I'm afraid I have some bad news. Your father was admitted to the hospital last night, initially for chest pains."

"What?" Marisa mind was spinning out of control. She had to get dressed quickly. She had to end this call and call her father fast. She needed to talk to him – now!

"Just tell me what hospital he's in, I'll be right there," Marisa said, her voice out of breath.

"Your father had a massive heart attack. I'm very sorry ... but he didn't survive."

Marisa fell back against the kitchen counter. This could not be happening. A massive heart attack? Didn't survive? "No!" Her voice was near hysteria. "No. No. No. I don't believe you!" She was sure the doctor was wrong. Her father couldn't be dead. He was mistaken. This was just a terrible nightmare, she would wake up, and everything would be fine.

"Mrs. McKenzie, we did everything we could ..."

Chapter Twenty-Two

Charlie Taft was buried in a cemetery plot next to his wife, Cassie. Marisa was an orphan now. This valley had taken those she loved one by one, and now she wondered, who would be next.

Marisa would never forgive herself for the last words she ever spoke to him, in anger, "Go home dad!"

Several days after the funeral, Marisa sat slumped in a chair and her once hot cup of tea had now gone tepid. Wearing gray sweat pants and a maroon Santa Rita sweatshirt, she hadn't even cared that she left the house with no make up on.

"You don't look very 'Saratoga' today my dear," Linda said jokingly.

The two best friends would laugh regularly about the so-called, "Saratoga Look." When a new family moved to town, the wife would be sized up quickly by the long-timers without her knowledge. The long-timers could tell just by looking at her, the way she dressed, the car she drove, her makeup, whether she'd "fit in" or not. Today Linda was trying to bring a smile to her friend's face only it wasn't working.

"You say something?" Marisa said, twirling a cinnamon stick around the brown water in her teacup. The café in the heart of the Saratoga Village was bustling at this time of morning, and Marisa didn't care if she'd gone out in public in sweats, that her hair was pulled into a ponytail, or that she had no make up on.

"You're bound to feel down. I mean, come on, and look what you've been through. Your raising the twins – practically by yourself, your husband is always working, and your father just passed away. I mean you've got a lot on your plate right now.

"I'll be fine … really." Marisa took a tube of lipstick and a compact out of her purse, stared into the tiny mirror and applied the lipstick, transforming her full lips from a natural hue to cherry red.

"That's a little bright for this time of morning, isn't it, what's up?"

Marisa stared out the café window and watched as perfectly coiffed women walked with babies in strollers and the steady stream of cars going down Big Basin Way. She didn't know why she hadn't cancelled her weekly coffee with Linda; she was in no mood to talk.

Linda reached into her purse and handed Marisa a business card. "Here's the name of Dr. Wells, she's an excellent therapist."

"I don't know, I can't go to a stranger," she said as she grabbed her purse to get up and leave.

"Just keep her number, call her when you're ready. With everything you've been through, it might be a good idea to talk to a professional."

"I'll think about it. Talk to you later."

She wouldn't call the therapist; she wasn't crazy, just a little lost. She was depressed, and under the circumstances, like Linda said, who wouldn't be?

Driving home, she made a detour and found herself in the parking lot of Saint Luke's Church. Getting out of the car, she glanced up at the large cross that towered over the property. She hoped her pastor would give her some free words of wisdom. Why should she pay for a therapist when Father Michael was available?

After all, he was there for his people. Just like Jesus. He was a representative of the Lord, and he would surely help her.

She turned the doorknob of the Parish's Office door and found it locked. She knocked but there was no answer. She knocked louder, and still no answer. As she waited, she thought how she came to the church office for committee meetings, but had never gone there for her own counseling, but that would soon change. She glanced around and saw Father Michael looking out his office window.

Someone finally came to the door. It was the parish secretary. She opened a small peephole and spoke through it. "Hello, Mrs. McKenzie, may I help you?"

"I'd like to talk to Father Michael."

"Is he expecting you today?"

"No," Marisa dabbed a tissue at her eyes. "No, he's not expecting me. No, I don't have an appointment. And no, I didn't call ahead." Marisa could feel herself losing her temper. "I just wanted to talk to him about something … something personal."

"Well," the secretary said with a sigh. "It's his day off, I don't know if he's available."

Knocking on the priest's half-open door with trepidation, the secretary stuck her head in. "Father

Michael, I'm sorry to bother you. I know it's your day off and all, but there's someone who wants to see you."

"You're right it is my day off, and I am busy, catching up."

"You're right, and I do apologize, but this woman seems a bit distressed, and Father Tony is out of the office."

Father Michael leaned back in his chair putting his hands behind his head. His parishioners were an upscale lot, wealthy people who always had some crisis it seemed; whether it be getting their child into the parish grammar school, high school or college; whether they wanted tickets for an audience with the Pope in Rome or an annulment without *true* cause. Whatever it was, his flock came to *him* whenever they wanted something, but where were *they* for Mass every week?

"Who is it that wants to see me?"

"Marisa McKenzie."

"Tell her to wait."

The pastor did a quick run through the financial records, stopping at the McKenzie family.

"On second thought," he said, "please tell her I'm not here."

The secretary returned with a solemn look on her face. "I'm sorry. He can't see you today."

"Is there someone else I could talk to?"

"No. The other pastor is out right now."

Great, Marisa said, leaving in a hurry. Under her breath, she mumbled. "I guess I don't give enough money to this Goddamned place."

The priest picked up a piece of paper from his in-box, and a smile crossed his face as he studied the list of new alter boys.

Chapter Twenty-Three

Someone pressed the intercom button outside the wrought iron gate of the Lawson estate, and Cora glanced at the screen of the security monitor. She told her maid she would respond to *this visitor*. At first thought there was no way she would let her in but decided she'd tell this tramp off for the last time. She pressed a button, the gate opened and the car pulled up the long driveway.

Cora opened the front door and before her stood Angela holding a dark haired baby girl. Nodding to her infant, she said the two words that would confirm her worst suspicions. "She's Philip's."

Cora had heard the company gossip but ignored it and now the idle gossip was standing right here in front of her.

"Do you mind if I come in?" Angela said as she pushed her way past Cora.

Cora went into the kitchen and reached into a cabinet where she kept a supply of anti-anxiety pills. Taking a glass of bourbon, a bit early in the day for some, but this was no ordinary day, she swallowed several pills and her stomach warmed though her head clouded.

"You've fixed this place up really nice."

"Is that what you came here to talk about, interior decorating?"

No, but if Cora left Philip, all this would be hers; if not, she'd still have enough money from her child's sperm donor to buy her own fabulous place.

"What do you want?" Cora asked bluntly. There was no way Angela Bowman was going to walk into her house and steal her life. She was merely a blip on a radar screen. She was like a gnat that needed to be squashed beyond recognition.

The pills kicked in: Cora refrained her desire to chokehold Angela. She should have seen this coming. She was experienced in this game. Knew the rules. Knew the game, and this was one game she was not prepared to lose. The first thing she needed to do was to get Angela out of her kitchen, out of her house, and out of her life.

Cora eyed Angela as she glanced around her house with a greedy look in her eyes. She imagined Angela to be picturing herself *residing in her home.*

The gloves were off. Cora swallowed the last of the bourbon in her glass, and walked over to look directly into Angela's eyes. "Get the Hell out of my house!"

Philip was meeting with a business reporter with long legs and large breasts who was interviewing him for a featured article.

While he answered her questions, he daydreamed into her pretty blue eyes and wondered about what sex would be like with her. His thoughts and interview was cut short by the persistent ringing of his cell phone.

"Can you either turn that off or answer it?"

"Shit," he said under his breath. Not only was his train of thoughts interrupted for the interview but now his libido was as well. Dammit.

"Lawson here."

"Get home now!"

The stern tone in Cora's voice told him he needed to cut this lunch date short. "An emergency just came up. Can we reschedule?" He grinned wide as he winked at the blonde-haired reporter.

"Sure."

"Call my secretary. Maybe next time we can meet at my condo in the city."

"That would be fine." She had heard of Philip's infamous condo in the city. Rumors were rampant about how he would take women there for cocktails and lovemaking. "Make it soon though, I'm on deadline."

"Sure," he said as he quickly left the restaurant.

Philip drove north on Highway 101 toward his Atherton home and reminisced about how much his life had changed.

Angela drove south on Highway 101 to her dingy apartment but with a smile on her face as she thought how much her life was going to change.

As Philip walked into the house, he wondered what was so important that couldn't wait until he got home from work that evening.

Philip spent hours talking with Cora in one of the hardest deals he ever negotiated. Finally, they struck an agreement. He would never admit Angela's baby to be his. Privately he could screw whomever he pleased but every night, he would come home to her. They would continue the pretense of a happily married couple; continue to live together as a couple, go out socially but privately he would have to reign in his testosterone level and use condoms, never putting Cora through this kind of pain again. She still wanted Philip. Sure, she did not need his *money* but she would not be humiliated by his actions – ever again.

"Get that memo sent out yet?" Cora asked.

Philip was sitting at his desk in his home office. "Yes, it's been sent, Angela has been officially terminated from the company. And I spoke with my attorney, he'll keep the paternity test confidential."

"I should certainly hope so. Oh, and there's one other thing ..."

Philip put his feet up on his desk and his hands behind his head. He was annoyed, what more did his wife want? "What is it?"

She leaned over the desk and her eyes blazed as if they penetrated his flesh. "If you think I'm done with you, you're wrong – dead wrong ..."

Angela sang to the baby, as she got closer to her apartment where Jack was waiting. He reminded her of a gold fish swimming in a tank, swimming in circles yet never going anywhere.

"I have something to tell you," Angela said as she walked into the apartment. "About Alexandra."

"Is she okay?" He had a concerned look on his face as he nervously finger combed his brown hair and furrowed his eyebrows. "What is it?"

"She's fine, there's nothing wrong with her. That's not it."

"What is it then?"

"Let me just put her down for a nap and I'll be right back." Angela put Alexandra in her crib, which she was soon to outgrow, and kissed her on the forehead before going out to the living room to face her soon to be ex-husband.

"Jack, I have something I've wanted to tell you for a long time."

"I don't like the sound of this."

"It's about Alex."

"So you said." Jack reached over and put his hands on Angela's wrists holding them tight. "Look me in the eyes and tell me what it is – now!"

"Okay. Okay. I'll just spit it out it. Philip is her father."

"What?"

"He's her biological father. And I'm going to file a paternity case against him."

"Oh, let me guess, this is about money?" Jack put his hands up to his face covering it in disbelief. Then he glared at her. "That's all you ever cared about was money, or finding a way to get your claws into some. Well you must be really proud of yourself. You really hit the jackpot this time."

In the other room, Alexandra started to cry, and Jack went to get her, turning to Angela. "Do you even care about her, or was she just a pawn in the game you're playing?"

"Of course I care about her." Angela fidgeted as she twirled a strand of her long hair around her finger.

"And how could you lie to me, pretend I was her father, all along you were probably laughing at me behind my back. How could you?"

"Darling," her voice came out patronizing though she hadn't intended it to be. That was just the way she spoke whether she meant to or not. *"You are her father, just not her blood father.* She has a biological father who can provide her with things you never could."

Jack's face turned from red to purple as he shouted. *"I'm not sure who to kill first, you or that bastard Philip Lawson!"*

Chapter Twenty-Four

Marisa loved this time of the year and did not mind driving on this freeway. A road sign declared it, THE MOST BEAUTIFUL FREEWAY IN THE WORLD, and she agreed. The caramel colored parched hills lining Highway 280 was a majestic sight.

She turned off onto curvy Magdalena Drive, which led to palatial estates tucked away like hidden jewels.

Marisa parked in an oval at the end of the long drive. After taking a deep breath, she climbed up the outside stairs that led to Dr. Wells' second story office.

Marisa knocked on the door, skeptical, but hopeful that Dr. Wells could help her.

The therapist shook Marisa's hand and welcomed her into a rose colored office. Her office had a feminine, yet powerful feel to it. Fresh gardenias in a crystal vase added a sweet scent to the room.

"Have a seat," Dr. Wells said as she motioned Marisa to sit down.

Dr. Wells sat in a light colored leather chair directly across from her new patient.

"Did you have any problem finding my office?"

"No, not at all."

"What brings you here today?"

"I've been having a hard time lately."

"I'm sorry to hear that."

Marisa looked down, unsure of what to say next.

"Would you like to tell me about it?"

Marisa looked at Dr. Wells. The therapist had a soft-spoken manner to her that made Marisa feel comfortable, at ease, as if she could tell her anything, if only she could get the words out.

"I really don't know where to begin."

"Well, tell me, who is Marisa McKenzie?"

Tears welled up in Marisa's eyes.

"Here," Dr. Wells said, handing Marisa a new box of tissues.

Marisa did not know why she was crying. All she knew was that she told Dr. Wells everything. She told her, her whole life story. She told her about her life from when she was a gardener's little girl right up to her high society madness.

She told her of her troubles with Josh, her mother's death, Johnny's death, and now the death of her father. She told her of her miscarriage. She told her she thought she wanted the life she saw looking through windows, but now she wasn't sure. It wasn't what she thought it would be. She just wanted to be herself, and just share the love with her husband and children, but she was confused.

By the time her session was over, Marisa felt invigorated by just releasing her feelings to another soul. She felt ready to take on the world. She was so engrossed in her thoughts that she didn't see the person coming up the stairs.

"Whoa, little lady," he said, as she bumped into him, knocking his cowboy hat off.

"Where you going in such a hurry," he said as he picked up his hat.

"I'm so sorry," she said.

"That's quite all right Ma'am."

Dr. Wells came rushing out of her office.

"I'm so sorry," she said to the cowboy. "I need to reschedule your appointment. An emergency just came up. Do you mind?"

"No," he said. "I'll just see you next week."

"Thank you so much," Dr. Wells said as she headed for her Jaguar.

"Well," the cowboy said to Marisa, "She sure was in a hurry."

"Yeah, she was …" Marisa subconsciously wiped under her eyes wondering if her mascara had smeared. "They say Dr. Wells is the best though," Marisa said, getting her car keys out of her purse. She headed for her car and he headed for his Jeep. The fiery sun was quickly and quietly finding a resting spot behind the rolling hills.

Marisa turned the ignition key of her car and started the engine. She caught a glance of herself in the rear view mirror. She didn't know if it was the release of emotions from her meeting with Dr. Wells, but she turned the key off.

She wanted to find the peace that Dr. Wells spoke of. She let out a sigh got out of her car and walked towards the short wooden fence that separated a pasture scattered with enormous oak trees.

Removing her shoes, Marisa sat on the wooden fence and dangled her legs over it. She wanted to savor every moment. The long green grass that kept the horses in the distance fed tickled her bare toes.

Dr. Wells had recommended to her that she needed to learn to enjoy the moment. She looked at her watch. The girls would be home from ballet practice soon. At least it was not her day to drive. Thank God for small favors. Thank God for car pools. Then said aloud, "Thank you God."

The cowboy approached her. "Did ya' say something?"

"Oh. I thought you'd left," Marisa said, a little embarrassed that she had been talking to herself.

"I thought you left!" he mimicked her.

"You know what?"

"What?" She asked.

"I haven't done this in years."

"What's that?"

"Just taking a minute."

Marisa smiled. That's exactly what she was doing, and it was not bad.

"Mind if I join you?"

"No, not at all …"

Together they watched the ball of fire descend below the mountains. One by one, the stars lit up the ever-darkening sky. They sat in silence and revered the beauty. She should have been nervous, sitting there with a stranger. However, she was not. She did not know how much time had gone by. They sat, talked, and admired the surrounding beauty.

A spiritual calmness descended upon her. Finally, Marisa said she "had to go." She had kids to feed, and a husband to keep happy. She had lunches to make. Schedules to keep. She had her life. Feeling renewed, Marisa started walking towards her car.

"Wait," the cowboy yelled after her. "I just want to thank you."

"What for?"

"Why for your precious time of course."

Marisa giggled. "You are most welcome!"

"Here's my card," he said. "If I can ever return the favor, just call."

"Thanks," Marisa said as she slipped his card in her purse.

Marisa arrived home to find the girls fed, bathed, and best of all, asleep. Josh was sleeping soundly on the sofa. He had such an innocent look to his face. A warm feeling came over her as she thought about the deep bond they shared. She visualized into the future and a smile crossed her face as she thought about what a perfect couple they made. Imagining her and Josh growing old together was easy. Even though they had difficulties on their roller coaster ride through life, their sacrosanct love went so deep she couldn't imagine anything ever disjoining their union. She leaned down and gave him a butterfly kiss on his cheek. For a moment, he opened his eyes. "I love you," he whispered.

"I love you too. Why don't go crawl into bed and I'll join you in a bit."

"Okay darling," he said sleepily.

She ran a warm sudsy bath, lit some aromatherapy candles, and submerged herself in dreams of long ago.

Chapter Twenty-Five

Angela had been in a good mood because her life was continuing as planned but negativity was permeating her being because she hated the drive from the South Bay to San Francisco, though it was only less than an hour's drive. She was low on gas. She hated that there were never any gas stations in the city; she didn't know how people lived there, the entire city was like a bee's nest, filled with insects flying about in a frenzy. It wasn't somewhere she wanted to live. She was going to take her baby and live elsewhere. She never saw Jack again after he ran out of the house in such a hurry. He'd be calling soon for her to send him his belongings, that she was sure, but she planned on being long gone by then, that's for sure.

She road up the elevator to the seventeenth floor and marveled at the view. The lawyer's office had a beautiful view of the Bay Bridge and on this day, it even included a few sailboats strung out across the choppy water.

On the attorney's desk were two things, legal documents for her to sign and a cashier's check for one million dollars.

The paternity tests proved that Philip Lawson was in fact Alexandra's biological father. An agreement had been reached. In exchange for one lump cash payment, Angela Bowman would relinquish all claims to Philip Lawson as Alexandra's father.

Philip needed his wife's money and the only way Cora would stay married to him, was if he severed ties with his illegitimate child. That was one humiliation, she had emphatically said, she would not suffer.

Philip's signature was already on the documents. He signed away all claims to the child. In a way, he felt sad because he had always wanted a daughter.

Chapter Twenty-Six

Joshua came home from work early looking dejected and disheveled. "I've been unable to secure the funding for the new company I wanted to start."

"I've tried and tried, but I can't get in to see Palmer."

Marisa put the wooden spoon down that she was using to stir the spaghetti sauce and turned to him. "Who's that?"

"David Palmer, the VC, the venture capitalist, he's the guy with the money."

"Oh ... well, I'm sure it'll all work out."

"Yeah ... someday ..."

The next day Marisa took her car to be washed and came out with much more than a clean car.

"I found this on the floor of your car." The car wash attendant said to her as she handed him his tip.

Marisa took the business card and read it. It was the one that the cowboy had given her. DAVID PALMER, VENTURE CAPITAL CONSULTANT.

Marisa made a quick phone call and a few minutes later she was driving up to Palo Alto to see the cowboy who now had a name to his rugged handsome face, a valuable name at that.

In an office on Sand Hill Road, with a view of the San Francisco Bay on one side and the famed Stanford University Tower on the other, Marisa waited to see him.

A few minutes later, Wanda, his secretary led her into his inner sanctum. Glancing around his office, she wondered if Dr. Wells had ever asked him, "who is David Palmer?"

David was thrilled to see Marisa but at the same time, wondered what she was doing there.

"I'm surprised to see you," he said, adding, "but really glad too."

She blushed. "I found your card in my purse and wanted to talk to you about a business proposal."

"Well, there's nothing like getting straight to your point," he laughed.

Her ruddy cheeks were now even more of a deep blush and she turned away from looking at him.

"Hey," he said, walking toward her. "We have a lot in common. After all, we have the same therapist!"

Marisa laughed as she felt her tension release.

"All I do is talk business, day and night," David said. "What do you say we take a break from all that – just for a little while."

"Okay, sounds fine to me. What did you have in mind?" Marisa was wondering what she'd gotten herself in for. What was she doing here? But she knew perfectly well what her plan was. If she could get David's backing, Josh would be able to be free from the snake Philip, and at last they'd have their own pot of gold. She supposed like everyone else who came to see David Palmer that she too had an ulterior motive. And David could see right through her.

"You probably want to see me about funding of some sort. I'm just guessing of course. But I've been around long enough to know people and what makes them tick. And I think you and I have three things in common."

"What's that?" Marisa asked, curious.

"I think we each have our own haunting demons, if you don't mind me being so bold, and we both want to find peace – inner peace. Why else would you have been at Dr. Wells' office?"

"What's the third thing?" Marisa asked, wondering if it had been a mistake coming here.

"The third, I'll tell you over a picnic lunch."

David told Wanda he was going to be in a meeting all afternoon, and he and Marisa went for a drive in his four-wheel drive Jeep.

Stopping at a deli, they picked up a bottle of wine and sandwiches, which they ate while they sat in a quiet park on a blanket and talked, and watched the horses grazing nearby.

"Like I was saying," David said. "I think we could both use a friend. This valley is filled with people who are your so-called friend one day, and the next, your enemy. It's like warfare, you can't let your guard down for one minute."

Marisa thought about Johnny. He lived through war only to come home and be killed.

"What is the point?" Marisa whispered.

"The point is," David said, "is we all want to be accepted, and we think money will get us what we all yearn for. We think money will make us better than the next guy. We all want to drive the fastest, hottest car, have the biggest house, the trophy spouse, the biggest IPO in valley history, we all want validation for our own being. Somewhere along the line, people have gotten their values screwed up." David shook his head. "Sorry, I didn't mean to go off on a tangent like that."

"No, that's okay. You're right, but I'm afraid I'm guilty as charged. I want all those things." Marisa's voice got quiet as she added, "and more ..."

"Yup, I could see it in your eyes. You have the fire. You have it in you to do whatever it takes to get ahead."

"Well, yeah," Marisa said. "But I'm not embarrassed about wanting things, why should I be? So I want the best schools for my kids, so I want a big house. I grew up without money, and yes, now I want it."

"I can see that."

David thought that he and Marisa had a lot in common. Marisa told him about her love for Joshua, but how confused she had been lately. He told her about his first girlfriend he ever had and how she reminded him of her.

She gently placed her head on his chest and they stayed until the sun set and the bottle of wine was gone. She saw him every day for the next few weeks. They never made love; they just held hands, talked, and went for long walks. They agreed on a platonic relationship. They needed someone to talk to, someone that didn't cost a hundred dollars a session. They would talk business soon enough, but for now they enjoyed each other's company.

When Marisa did tell him about the Zanex proposal it was done properly, not on a picnic blanket or on horseback, but in his office. She made an appointment through Wanda and went to his office wearing her best business attire.

Marisa explained the business proposal to him, in detail. She told him how she had originally thought of the Zanex idea while she was attending college years earlier, but that because of the trauma of her brother dying, and then going to college and marrying and having children, she got sidetracked. She told him she thought it was a good idea, but she had set it aside to raise a family and help her husband succeed.

Marisa told him how she had given the idea to Joshua and how he had been unable to get through to him. She explained that she did not want anything to do with the company; she just wanted Joshua to succeed, while she stayed in the background.

David was impressed with Marisa's knowledge for business and told her she seemed to have missed her calling. He said she had a real vision of her ideas. He told her if she ever wanted to leap into the business world, to give him a call. In addition, he told her not to worry about the funding, as far as he was concerned, it was a done deal.

"The money came through," Josh told Marisa, calling from the new silver-colored Porsche sports car he had just leased after the successful meeting with Palmer.

"I'm so proud of you. I told you that you didn't need Philip."

Josh's stomach felt hollow. He had not told Marisa the truth. That he had included Philip on the deal. Unlike Marisa, Josh had faith in Philip - after all, he was his mentor.

After the newly formed Zanex received the influx of venture capital, courtesy of David Palmer, Philip and Joshua moved forward and set up the company. They would hire many Lawco employees, and Josh left it to Philip to run the day-to-day operations. He was unaware however, that Philip had plans of his own for Zanex.

Once the company was off the ground and running, Philip was going to change the executive structure. Driving in his new red Ferrari, he made a phone call -- to Joshua. "Josh, you understand, it's just business, the VCs want new people at the helm." He grinned as he thought how easy it was for him to lie. Joshua was always so naive and gullible; he would believe anything. Philip knew the way the Valley worked. He knew the correlation between business, loyalty and friendship - there wasn't any. Loyalty in Silicon Valley ran as deep as the shallow friendships it created.

"What are you talking about?" Josh could not believe what Philip was telling him.

"Josh, *you* want what's best for the company, right? You just aren't part of the package."

"That can't be right, I met with Palmer myself. He knew I was part of the deal – that it was *my deal.*"

"He changed his mind. I just got off the phone with him. Sorry Josh." Philip's lies even surprised himself; he'd been telling falsehoods for so long he spoke as if even he believed them.

Josh could not believe how callously Philip cut him out. How easily the cold-hearted words came to the ruthless bastard. *Philip Lawson and his greed was one class that was not covered in business school.*

"I need to talk to David immediately," Josh said.

"I'm sorry, he's in conference." Wanda had covered for her boss so many times she soon learned it was easier to tell people he was simply in a conference.

"I need to talk to him. It's an emergency."

"He's out of the office in a meeting and he won't be back today. Can I leave a message for you?"

"Yes, tell him to fuck off!"

Josh decided not to tell Marisa about Philip's cutting him out of the deal, not yet. He would first find a way to get himself back in, he had to, Marisa thought he was doing the deal on his own, and if she found out not only he was cut but that Philip was involved, there was no telling what she'd do.

Chapter Twenty-Seven

Marisa decided the time had come to go through the metal box that she had found in her father's house after he had died. She drove over the hill and stopped at Castle Rock Park. There was no other place to open the metal box except on top of the mountain that reached for the stars. The same mountain, where Marisa and Johnny spent so many carefree days, the one place they could go and be free. Except that now, she was not feeling that sense of freedom.

Glancing at the sky she contemplated if Johnny, her mother and father were watching over her, if they knew how much she ached inside. She wondered if they knew, how very much she missed them, how much she loved them. Thinking of her family brought her a desire to embrace and discover her heritage like she'd never experienced before.

Marisa sat on a smooth rock on the mountaintop, set the box on her lap, and took a deep breath and thought about what might be inside. She wondered if it would help her say goodbye. Goodbye to Johnny, and to her father and mother.

She wondered what secrets the box held. She opened it and took out some papers and a card that Marisa had drawn for her father when she was little. In a child's handwriting, drawn with a red crayon, it read, "I love u." She set the card aside and unfolded a note that was written in her mother's handwriting. "Charlie, thank you for rescuing me, I love you as deep as the ocean is blue, my heart is yours forever, love, Cassie."

Marisa searched for tissue to wipe away the tears that she couldn't stop even if she wanted to. She took one more thing out of the box, an envelope that had her brother's name on it. She held it against her chest and her heart was pounding as she opened it.

Marisa did not know the envelope existed until this moment. She had always felt a lost connection when Johnny died when part of her was lost forever. Holding in the memories of her brother from the night so long ago when he died.

She took a silk scarf from around her neck on placed it on her lap. Marisa took a deep breath and turned the envelope so the items inside fell onto her scarf.

Seventy-five cents in loose change fell from the envelope onto her now trembling legs. Amidst the coins was a silver plated lighter with a peace symbol on it, and a leather wallet.

Marisa looked inside the billfold, there were two crinkled five-dollar bills and two one-dollar bills. Pulling out Johnny's driver's license, his picture didn't do him justice, Marisa thought.

She looked in a small, almost hidden pocket inside the wallet and pulled out a small grainy black and white photograph. It was taken at the Boardwalk at Santa Cruz Beach, where they had spent so much time. Where they could go and there was no care how much or how little money a person had. Marisa smiled as she looked at the photograph. Her and Johnny in a moment of laughter caught forever on film.

Through her tears, she emptied the rest of the envelope. One more item fell out. A ring. It was a thick gold ring with a signet stone in the center. Marisa didn't remember Johnny ever wearing a ring; he didn't like wearing jewelry of any kind, especially an expensive looking gold ring.

Marisa held it and looked at the inside of the band. There were some markings on the inside band, but she couldn't tell what it said, her eyes were filled with tears as her vision blurred. She put the ring and the other items back in to the envelope and closed the metal clasp shut.

When she arrived home, she put the envelope away but kept the ring out and put it on a gold chain.

When Josh arrived home, he noticed the new piece of jewelry around her neck. "Where did you get that thing from?"

"I was going through a box of my brother's things today and found it. It was in an envelope. The police had gathered his effects from the scene of the accident and had given the envelope to my father."

"Can I see it?"

"Sure."

Josh looked at it carefully. "This ring could use a little cleaning, it could be brightened up and made good as new. Tell you what, I know how busy you are, I'll take it to the jewelers and have it as good as new."

"Oh, okay, that's sweet of you."

The next morning, Josh stopped at an exclusive jewelry store in nearby Los Gatos. He had a busy morning, meeting with lawyers over his rights to the Zanex deal, but this could not wait.

Over the next couple of weeks, Marisa asked Josh when the ring would be ready.

"I mean, how long does it take to clean a ring?"

"Soon," was all he would say.

Marisa loved Josh for taking the ring to be cleaned, but she couldn't wait any longer. She rang the door buzzer of the jewelry store. A balding man with bi-focal glasses perched on his head peered out the door.

The jewelry store was small and very exclusive, catering to the rich of the valley and kept its doors locked at all times, letting in an elite few.

"Yes, may I help you?"

"May I come in?"

"State your business."

"My husband, Josh McKenzie, left a ring here to be cleaned. And I wanted to see if it was done. I'd like to pick it up."

A buzzer sounded, the door unlocked, and Marisa was granted entry.

"Have a seat."

"And you said your name is McKenzie?"

"That's right."

Looking through a 3-ring binder with sales receipts in it, he prided himself on his organizational skills. "Mrs. McKenzie, it says here that the ring was picked up already."

"Oh" Marisa said, relieved. "My husband must've forgotten to tell me."

"Gosh, I gave your husband's ring back to him several days ago."

"Oh, I'm so sorry to bother you then, thank you so much for your time." Marisa got up from the chair." He probably wants to surprise me," she said. "Our anniversary is coming up."

Marisa was elated; soon, she would have her ring back, her brother's ring. She walked towards the door. "By the way, the ring belonged to my brother." Marisa sighed. "But he's gone now. He died in an accident."

"I'm sorry to hear that."

"Yes, me too"

When she arrived home, there was a message from the girls private school, wanting "Mr. or Mrs. McKenzie to call the business office immediately about the twins past due tuition."

Marisa confronted Josh about not paying the tuition when he arrived home. He wanted to spare Marisa the news, but decided he had no choice but to tell her the whole truth, or most of it, "I have bad news about Zanex and Philip Lawson. Philip has cut me out. They're moving full-steam ahead with the business but unfortunately as of now, I'm not a part of it. But don't worry, I'll sue his ass if it comes down to that."

Philip cutting Josh out did not surprise her. Normally she would have been up all night talking about it with Josh but that was the last thing on her mind. She thought about her past and her future and she came to the conclusion that since it was their anniversary coming up, Josh probably wanted to surprise her with the ring. She decided not to bother him again and just wait for him to give it to her as a gift.

In the meantime, she wanted answers, answers about Johnny's death. Her father would never talk about what happened the night Johnny died, and Marisa wanted the truth.

The next day she drove to the police station that handled her brother's accident case.

"I want to see the Officer that was in charge when my brother, Johnathan Taft was killed."

"You are in luck Ma'am," the man said behind the desk. "He is still on the force and he is in the office today. I'll call for him, have a seat in the waiting room and he'll be right out."

Marisa sat on a cold metal chair, waited, and pondered what had possessed her to go to the police station. She knew there was a chapter of her life that was incomplete that needed closure, her brother's death. When her mother died, she knew that she had had cancer, so it was not something that she questioned. Marisa understood about her father's death, he had had a heart attack, and she was to blame. It had been years since Johnny was killed. Nothing could change that – yet she had longed for the truth.

"I'm Detective McGrill. Can I help you?"

Marisa wondered how long he had been on the force. His black hair had streaks of silver interlaced and his face looked like he had smoked too many cigarettes all his life.

"Is there somewhere we can talk in private?"

"Sure, just follow me."

McGrill led her to an empty room. The walls had peeling lime green paint and fluorescent lights that made her eyes squint.

Marisa began slowly, "I want some information about--" It was all Marisa could do to get the words out. "The night my brother was killed."

McGrill excused himself to go get the old file folder that was still filed in "Cases Pending" drawer.

"Yes, I remember this case," he said as he briefly looked through the paperwork in the file folder.

"What I want to know is," Marisa began, "was there a ring that was in with my brother's possessions?" Then she stopped, unable to continue as tears filled her eyes and her throat tightened.

He gave her a tissue and she wiped the tears from her blood shot eyes and tried to continue. "There was a ring ..."

"Yes?" He was trying to understand what Marisa was doing there, but he knew it was not uncommon for relatives to search for answers years after a death of a loved one. He knew that certain events would trigger the desire for more knowledge of the circumstances surrounding the death. Especially in cases like this one, that remained unsolved. He was just looking forward to the day soon when he would be retiring and then he would not have to deal with grieving relatives anymore.

"Just take your time." He patted her on her hand and brought her a glass of water.

McGrill searched through the paperwork in the folder. He looked at the typed itemization list of the items that were found on Johnathan Taft and read through the list of personal affects. "Let's see, says here, seventy-five cents change. Silver lighter. Leather wallet filled with thirteen dollars, and one signet ring."

"But Sir", Marisa said, "About the ring, do you know anything about it, because I was surprised that my brother had a ring, especially an expensive gold ring, he never wore any jewelry."

He looked through the paperwork for a third time and excused himself from the room.

McGrill stammered upon his return. "Miss Taft, the ring was found among your brother's belongings, so I guess you just didn't know he had a ring."

He cleared his throat then took a sip of water before continuing, "Of course," he said in an off-handed tone, "Well, it is possible that the ring belonged to the driver of the hit and run."

"What are you talking about? How could that be?"

"Well, we're just officers, were not perfect, and I was just speculating."

Marisa left the police station in a hurry and sped home as fast as she could.

"I need the ring," she desperately told Josh as she entered the house.

"Well, hello to you too!"

"Just give me the ring."

"Marisa, sit down, "I didn't want to tell you this, but I accidentally lost the ring. *I don't know what happened.* I picked it up from the jewelry store, and the next I knew, it was missing. Maybe I lost it outside the store."

Marisa couldn't breathe. She thought she was having an asthma attack; only she didn't have asthma, at least not until now.

"I'll buy you another ring," Josh said, trying to make her feel better, trying to make up for her loss.

The next day, Marisa hurried to the jewelry store.

"What can I do for you?" The jeweler asked.

Her mind was spinning, her voice shaky, "I want to ask you about the ring my husband picked up. I just wanted to ask you about it because he said he lost it. I wanted to see if you found it, I think my husband said he might have dropped it outside of your store."

"What was your name again?"

"McKenzie, remember I was here the other day." Marisa continued, "I wanted to ask you about the ring my husband picked up."

"Oh yes, I remember, your husband's ring."

"No," Marisa said as she felt faint, "it was not my husband's ring."

"I wondered about that. I thought it was your husband's ring because he had brought it in for cleaning and repair work."

"Yes, he brought it in, but as I told you before, there was no repair work, just cleaning."

"Well, in any case, he was in a hurry to get it completed."

"He was getting it cleaned for me as a gift, for our anniversary." Marisa took a deep breath before continuing, "he felt terrible because he lost it outside the store here and it's very important that I find it."

The jeweler went on, "You know it's odd, it's the first time I've ever had someone in such a hurry to get engraving removed from a ring."

"Removed?"

"Yes, usually, people are in a hurry to get engraving on a ring, but he couldn't wait to get if off."

"I don't know what you're talking about. There was no engraving to be removed."

"There was a name."

"What name?"

The jeweler went to his binder, where he kept his receipts and records and looked it up. "Oh yes," he said, as he put his bifocals on. "The name he had removed was, Joshua McKenzie."

"That's impossible!"

The jeweler would not stop the words. Stop. He was torturing her and she did not know why.

"Joshua McKenzie," he repeated.

Marisa stumbled out of the door of the store and into her car, it was drizzling but she drove without turning on the windshield wipers. She knew she found herself parking in her driveway of her house but barely remembered driving home. She tried to make sense of it all. When she entered the house. Josh was waiting for her in the kitchen. On the table was a small turquoise box.

"Darling, guess what?"

Her raincoat dropped out of her hands and fell to the floor. "What?"

"The jewelry store found the ring. I had dropped it outside their store. Can you believe it?"

"No, I can't."

Josh picked up the box from the table and handed it to her. "Happy Anniversary!"

Marisa opened the box. Inside was *the ring*. She looked at the inside band. All traces of any engraved name had been removed. A perfect job. "I don't feel so good," she said, as she set the ring on the table and staggered to her bedroom, locking the door.

Chapter Twenty-Eight

Marisa spent the night in a state of shock. She told Josh she was getting a migraine and needed to be alone. She didn't tell him that she knew the truth. She couldn't talk to him, couldn't look at him. There was nothing to say. Marisa spent the night, knowing what she would do in the morning. She would wait for him to leave for the club, for his usual morning workout and then leave – for good. Of course she would leave him a note.

Her reverie was interrupted as the statuette she had been holding onto slipped from her fingers and fell onto the hardwood floor breaking into small pieces that she quickly swept into the corner of the room.

"Girls. Let's go."

With the car packed, they were off to a new life. A life filled with new attitudes, new experiences and new people to meet. New everything waited for them. But first, they had to leave Silicon Valley. It would not take them long to leave the silicon madness behind.

Chapter Twenty-Nine

Philip Lawson pushed his red Ferrari to its limit on the misty mountain highway. The only thing on his agenda for that morning was the sexy Realtor in the passenger seat next to him.

She was fully aware of his glances toward her full breasts that spilled out from her low-cut blouse. She would give this power-house full reign to her body once they got to the vacant estate overlooking the Pacific Ocean … once she got his signature on the Agreement to Purchase Property document.

He put his hand on Gina Maxwell's thigh and smiled as he thought about what the day would bring.

His life was planned down to the minute, but the one thing he had not planned on was when he turned a blind corner and a deer in the middle of the road. He tried to slam on the brakes but his foot went flush to the floor. His brakes didn't respond. The car spun around several times before it veered down a canyon and burst into flames. A passing motorist saw the blazing inferno and called 911.

David Palmer heard the news on the radio on his way in to work. "I'll be damned, they really went through with it."

He thought about turning the conspirators, the murderers, in to the police. But, *he* wasn't worth the time of day and *she* could be useful down the road. She would be willing to pay anything to keep him quiet, but it wasn't about money. It was the game, and he knew how to play. Everyone in the Valley harbored secrets, and he knew how to keep them too. Success in Silicon Valley depended on being in the right place at the right time – some win, others lose. Today he was going to create a winner, and keep someone else's secrets.

A week earlier

An unlikely trio of David Palmer, Cora Lawson and Jack Bowman had met at Buck's in Woodside.

"Let's go over the plan one more time," Cora said. "Jack, I'll give you the code to the gate and the garage where his car will be parked - you know what to do from there."

Taking a bite of a pancake with maple syrup dripping down his chin, Jack cocked his head at Cora. "Why don't you just get a divorce?" He wiped his face with the back of his hand and had a confused and puzzled look on his face.

"If you do as I say, in addition to your share of the million your whore of a wife got from me, you'll have your own million in cash."

Jack smiled at the thought of having that much money. He'd be able to do anything he wanted. He could quit his mail route, live the life of leisure, but most importantly fight Angela for custody of Alexandra. Living without his little girl brought him heartache. He decided he could live with the fact that he wasn't Alex's biological father but he couldn't live without her. He wanted Alexandra, at any cost. And he had wanted revenge against Philip and this opportunity had presented itself. "Okay," he said with a grin. "I'm in."

Palmer took a sip of coffee and set his mug down. "Cora, you sure you want to go through with this?"

Cora pushed her plate to the center of the table. "This has been a long time coming. He has humiliated me for the last time." She thought she could live with the fact that Angela had his child but she simply couldn't and wanted revenge.

"I know Cora but—"

"No buts David. How long have you and I known each other? How far back do we go?"

"Back to the early days, you know that."

"I helped you get your start, right here in this restaurant as a matter of fact, and I've never asked anything in return ... until now."

"I know that. But I can't, I won't be a part of this."

"Don't you want to help out your little girlfriend?"

"What are you talking about?"

"Marisa, of course. I know that Philip has been interfering with the Zanex deal." Cora now made it a point to know everything that went on with her husband.

"One, she's not my girlfriend. And two, there are other ways."

"It's not like we're gonna kill him, we'll just put a little scare into him, put him out of commission for awhile, that's all."

"Philip is toast. I can take care of him myself." David got up to leave. "Either way, I'll deny any knowledge that this conversation ever took place."

"Good. We all need to keep quiet." Cora snapped her fingers at a passing waitress. "Check please."

*   *   *

David thought about that day in the restaurant. He didn't think Cora and Jack would actually go through with it. But not being one to leave anything to chance, he was ready with his own plan, just in case.

Upon hearing the news of Philip Lawson's death, David immediately called his secretary and told her to set up an emergency Board of Directors meeting in a conference room of his office. The Board had assembled by the time he arrived.

"Hold all my calls," he told Wanda. "I'll be in conference."

"You mean that for once you'll *really* be in conference?"

"Very funny."

"I'll bring down some coffee and water."

"That'll be fine, but first, get Marisa McKenzie on the phone."

"I assume you've all heard the news about Lawson," Palmer said as he entered the conference room. "Too bad about the woman though, but we have important business to discuss. This new company we funded, Zanex, needs a temporary CEO."

"What about Josh McKenzie?"

"No." David said emphatically. "I have someone else in mind." He explained to the Board that he wanted someone who was familiar with the company and who could realize its vision. Although, it was someone who was not a typical Silicon Valley executive, by local standards, it was someone that he would break the mold; break with tradition, a fresh person with untainted desire. There was only one person for the job, Marisa McKenzie.

Chapter Thirty

Josh rode an exercise bicycle at the club with tears filling his eyes and one thing on his mind ... Marisa. He had seen her heart break when he told her the news of Zanex, but it didn't compare to the horror on her face when he gave her the ring. What had he been thinking? There was only one thing he could do. He quickly left the club and drove home, calling his lawyer on the way. "Let Philip have the damn company, I don't care anymore!" He had more on his mind than suing Philip Lawson, his long time mentor, more on his mind than Zanex. *More on his mind than Silicon Valley.*

Throwing out of the car window, his cell phone, and anti-anxiety pills, he had advised his lawyer to "get a life ... I'm going to!"

He would find a way to explain to Marisa. How when he was in college, he got drunk, and mindlessly drove his car for a liquor store run and accidentally hit a pedestrian. He stopped to check the severity of the injury, and was shocked to see that he was dead. In a panic, he left the scene. He had thought about turning himself in but he had plans for his life; he wanted success at any cost, even if it meant keeping secrets.

When he found Marisa again that fateful night at the fraternity party, he never knew the soul he took was her brother's. Not until she showed him the ring, the oversized signet ring that had slipped from his finger on that murderous night.

Now, as he thought about his past and his future, he only wanted Marisa by his side. Without her, life was meaningless.

He would go to the police station, but first, he had to see Marisa. When he arrived home and read the note that Marisa had left for him he raced to his car. The police could wait. His love for Marisa could not.

Chapter Thirty-One

Up the peninsula, in a mansion in Hillsborough, an elderly man lay dying. He was living on memories and borrowed time. Soon he would be joining his wife in heaven who died four years after their daughter, Cassandra left ... pregnant with Charlie Taft's child.

Over the years, James Thoroughgood continued his newspaper dynasty until his failing health caused him to sell all his business holdings, adding more millions to his overflowing bank account.

He had ceased all contact with his daughter, Cassandra, cutting her out of his will and his life, as he had warned her he would. Then when Charlie had called him and told him that she had passed away, he still could not bring himself to acknowledge her, even to attend her funeral. Over the years, he had remained stubbornly adamant in his feelings. Now, with time running out, remorse filled his soul. He could not change the past, but he could change someone else's future. He had contacted his attorney and had his will changed, leaving everything to his only grandchild, Marisa McKenzie.

Now as the minutes ticked away, he had one last wish ... to talk to his granddaughter, at least once. Pulling the oxygen tubes out of his nose, he whispered instructions to his nurse.

"Call her," he said, barely audible.

The nurse called but there was no answer.

"Try again ..."

"I'm sorry, Mr. Thoroughgood, I've tried her home several times but there's no answer."

James Thoroughgood's head fell to his chest as the last shallow breath was expelled from his lifeless body.

Chapter Thirty-Two

As Marisa's car climbed through the mountainous Grapevine leading to Los Angeles, her cell phone would not stop ringing.

Finally, she answered it.

"Hello?"

"Marisa, David Palmer here. I'll get right to the point. We want you to run Zanex."

"That's very flattering, David, and yesterday, that would've meant the world to me, but this is tomorrow and I have plans."

"Marisa, this is an opportunity of a lifetime."

"David, I don't want any part of it anymore. You know, I thought it would be different, but I was wrong." She *never* realized how quickly the land of silicon, the land of gold, could so easily turn into rust.

"We need people like you. *I need you.* Not people like Philip Lawson, besides, he won't be a problem anymore."

"What do you mean?"

"Haven't you heard? He's dead."

"Dead?" Marisa swerved into the other lane, narrowly missing a car. "Hold on a minute," she said, "I'm going to get off at the next exit." Pulling into a coffee shop parking lot, her mind raced.

"Are you listening to me?" David's voice through the cell phone was cutting in and out.

"I don't know …"

"Marisa, I won't take no for an answer!"

Before she could respond, she glanced in the rear view mirror and saw a car had pulled in behind her.

"David, I can't talk now. I'll have to call you back." She quickly headed out of the parking lot but it was too late, he had caught up with her. She had a life decision to make. Should she step on the gas or the brakes?

Chapter Thirty-Three

Two years later

An empty bottle of Dom Perignon floated upside down in a silver bucket of melted ice. Two champagne glasses slowly etched water circles into the top of the antique nightstand. The program from the SilVa Awards was on the floor along with the satin bedding.

Marisa's beaded dress, one she had purchased at a vintage thrift shop, remained on the bed, keeping her bare feet warm. When she got up, she passed by the award, and smiled. Winning the SilVa Award for "Entrepreneur of the Year," was a climax that only competed with sex that she realized she was ready for more of – with her husband.

He quietly came through the back door leading into the kitchen, carrying a stack of newspapers he had just gone out to purchase, with Marisa on the front page.

The following day would bring an interview on a national TV news program, hosted by Marisa's best friend, Linda MacGregor. Marisa was going to take the opportunity to announce a charitable foundation funded by the inheritance from her grandfather, James Thoroughgood. She was going to call it, The C&C Endowment Fund, in honor of her parents, Cassandra and Charlie.

Along her way through the Silicon Valley maze, Marisa found forgiveness in her heart and success in the boardroom. And with the man she loved she found a place in the Valley after all. She thought once she reached the pinnacle of success, her problems would go away. She thought that the people that lived inside the looking glass were somehow better than she was. She soon discovered when she was finally inside that the windows still needed cleaning.

Nothing could bring her brother or her parents back, but she grew to remember a day when she had met a boy who sat with her while she was awash with despair. She remembered a man who consoled her when she was wrought with grief, a man who saved her life. A man she loved.

That day on the Grapevine, when he had caught up with her, took her into his arms, held her tight, and kissed her with a passion he had never shown before, at first she resisted. Pushed him away. Told him she never wanted to see him again. That it was over.

Josh begged for her forgiveness and continued love. His voice was filled with desperation as he poured his heart out to her like he never had before. He had always held back from her and she never knew why. Now, she understood, he had been harboring an unforgivable secret.

But she did forgive him, even though she would never forget. She found forgiveness in her heart because of the undeniable bond she shared with Joshua. She remembered how he made her feel, the love they shared, and the children they created. Just as he had lost sight of her on his journey to the top, she too lost sight of what mattered most in life.

Marisa bounced downstairs wearing her favorite denim cut-offs and a white T-shirt. She would take the day off before going back to the work in the valley of dreams.

From the backyard of their new house on Overlook Point, they had a commanding view of the valley. They embraced as they looked over to the ridge where they had met for the first time in the blue hills of Saratoga. Marisa now had everything she had ever wanted. And it was good. The material things did not internally change her life as she always thought it would. She thought it ironic that when she actually obtained the much sought after possessions validating success, she realized it was only a matter of perception. The words her father so often spoke, ran through her head ... "Money does not your heart make." She now understood the meaning. The love in your heart makes you whole and it had been there all along.

Photo credit: Bob Hsiang

About the Author

As a young child, Catherine Burr moved with her family from Canada to sun-drenched Northern California. With her siblings, she played in the orchards and open fields of Santa Clara Valley, cherishing the beauty of the land, until progress arrived in the name of Silicon Valley. When her father took her on a tour of an early Silicon Valley computer company, she was filled with intrigue, as the framework was being laid for the high-tech generation, as well as ideas for Catherine's future novels.

When Catherine's two sons started college, she decided to fulfill her dream of writing fiction. *Desires and Deceptions* is Catherine's second published novel. Catherine is also the author of *Silicon Secrets*, and co-author of the parenting humor book, *Motherhood is not for Wimps*. In addition, her short stories are published the anthology book, *Misadventures of Moms and Disasters of Dads*, and the *Wreal Writers Write Romance* audio book.

Besides writing, Catherine enjoys gardening, curling up with a good book, and the beach. Catherine is currently at work on her next novel.

Visit Catherine's website at www.catherineburr.com

NEW LINE PRESS

To order additional copies
of this book or Silicon Secrets

Visit the New Line Press website

www.newlinepress.com

Read Catherine Burr's first novel,
Silicon Secrets

Lucky arrives in Silicon Valley ready to strike it rich
but is sidetracked by two beautiful women. What's a guy to do?

SILICON SECRETS
Trade Paperback
ISBN 1-892851-01-6

Silicon Secrets, Catherine Burr's award-winning debut novel,
has been called, "Smoldering" by My Shelf Book Reviews,
"Highly recommended" by Midwest Book Review and "Sexy"
by the Sacramento Bee.

Also Visit Catherine Burrs's website

www.catherineburr.com